D1380476

Chapter One

It was the kind of day I liked best in the library. The building was full of students working on group projects, readers hanging out in the armchairs by the fireplace, and lots of little kids with their parents looking at picture books. Fitz, our library cat, was curled peacefully on the desk near me and glancing around the library with the same look of satisfaction that I'm sure I sported on my own face.

What was more, the equipment was all working smoothly. The computers throughout the building were running without a hitch, and even our finicky copier machine was on its best behavior. It was ordinarily the kind of copier that had multiple shenanigans a day (sometimes because of clueless patrons, but sometimes because the machine simply felt mischievous).

We were also well-staffed, so I wasn't having to work the circulation desk and check out patrons' books, but instead could be stationed at the reference desk.

I decided to spend my time unpacking the shipment of new books that had come in that morning. Seeing the new materials always made me smile, and it also gave me ideas for my own reading list. Processing the new books meant separating them into piles—some of the new titles needed to go to borrowers who had already requested the book.

I was unpacking new books for our fiction collection and one of them made me pause. I looked at the name on the cover and then flipped over to the back of the book.

"Something wrong with the shipment?"

I looked up to see my director, Wilson, standing there. I must have seemed confused because Wilson explained, "You were frowning."

"Oh, it's this book." I handed it over to Wilson, who studied it carefully through his rimless glasses.

"It's on the bestseller list, I know," he said slowly. "I've heard about it." He flipped the novel over to the back. "The author looks familiar. Have we had her in here to speak?"

I said, "She's actually one of our regular patrons."

Wilson took a closer look and slowly nodded. "Right. So her name is Sally Simmons. Sits over there, doesn't she?" He waved vaguely toward the quiet study area in the far corner. He frowned, trying to remember more. "Wears a scarf, doesn't she? I kept wondering if the air in the library was too chilly."

I nodded. "She does wear a scarf—it looks homemade. I thought she was a grad student, or someone studying for a professional certification of some sort. She comes in with her laptop and is over there for hours in the quiet area."

"Have you spoken much with her?"

"No, she keeps to herself. She always seems like she has a lot to do. She rarely stops by the desk. But I've seen her in here for months," I said. I thought some more. "Actually, it could have been more than a year."

Wilson handed the book back to me. "The novel is extremely well-reviewed. Let's have her in here for an author event. She can speak, then we can have an audience Q&A."

"And a signing?"

"I suppose so," said Wilson. He was less fond of signings.

"Should we have refreshments? I think the budget will allow for them."

Wilson was often rather tight with his budget but seemed to be picturing a large event this time. "Definitely. But let's do it on the economical end. A fruit tray, pastries, coffee, that type of thing. Light snacks."

"Got it. I'll try to find contact information for Sally online."

Wilson glanced over at the door. "Or just wait for her to come in."

Sure enough, Sally was slipping through the door now. It was a testament to how frequently she was here that Wilson and I remembered her because she was a very inconspicuous person. She had dull sandy-blonde hair that she kept in a long, loose braid. And she was again wearing that homemade scarf. Perhaps she was very cold-natured.

I was about to move to the other side of the reference desk to catch up with her, but Wilson was a few steps ahead of me.

He called out, "Ms. Simmons."

Sally stopped and turned, looking a bit combative for some reason as I joined Wilson.

Wilson continued, "We've just gotten a shipment of new books, and yours is one of them. We're thrilled to have a best-selling author in our library."

Sally relaxed a little, although she still looked wary. "Thanks." A thin hand worried at the fringe on her scarf.

Wilson looked expectant, as if thinking she might continue, but apparently Sally wasn't much in the mood to talk. He blinked and pushed his glasses farther up his nose. "Did you work on the book here in the library?"

Sally nodded. "That's right."

Wilson glanced at me. Since I've worked with him for years, I could tell what he was thinking. Would Sally be this taciturn during a library event? It boded ill for a talk if that were the case.

I cleared my throat. "I'm Ann and this is Wilson, my library director. We were wondering if you might be interested in us hosting an author event here at the library."

Considering how short she'd been with her replies, I was thinking that her answer was going to be a quick no. But Sally's eyes lit up.

"Here?" She glanced around the stacks.

Wilson seemed relieved at Sally's reaction. "The event would actually be in our community room here. It's a nice space, seats a fair number of people, and can adapt well for any type of talk. You could even hold a multimedia presentation there. Ann and I were just talking about the possibilities. We could offer some light refreshments for the attendees, have you speak a bit about yourself, your book, and your writing process, and then open it up to a question-and-answer session. Would that be something you might be interested in?"

Sally blinked at him with her big eyes. "Next week?"

"Well, we'd want to push it out a little longer than that, to give ourselves the opportunity to promote it," said Wilson. "That way we could get a nice crowd here."

Fitz trotted over to join us. He stopped in front of Sally, gazing solemnly at her.

She reached down and rubbed his fur.

"I see you know Fitz," I said cheerfully.

Sally nodded, still looking down at the cat. "He comes over and visits me in the quiet area. He sits in my lap sometimes while I'm typing."

I smiled. "It sounds a little awkward. Does he interfere with your writing?"

"He relaxes me, actually. I get more done when Fitz is around."

Wilson looked impatient, ready to get the event locked down so that he could return to whatever paperwork he'd left to begin with. "Do you think having an event two weeks from now would work? On a Monday. That should give us enough time to get the word out and plan everything."

Personally, I thought that was cutting it close, but I bit my tongue.

Sally considered this, and then carefully brought out her cell phone to check her calendar. "That will work out fine." She paused. "You'll be reaching out to the community, you said?"

Wilson nodded. "Ann here is a whiz with promotion. She has Fitz take part as part of her social media campaigns, and her posts get shared a lot more."

Fitz gave a complacent feline smile, as if realizing the job he did was very important. Sally rubbed the cat again, and he raised his head so that she could scratch him under his chin.

Wilson said, "If you could, please give Ann your contact information so we can be in touch closer to time with more details. We're looking forward to it."

As Wilson strode back toward his office, Sally quickly provided her contact details. I'd sort of figured she'd pass the time with me for a few minutes, but she seemed eager to retreat to the quiet study area. "Thanks," she said in a gruff voice and then disappeared into the stacks.

Fitz watched her as she went, as if thinking he wanted to follow her, but realizing she wanted to be alone. I settled myself back behind the reference desk and reached out to Fitz, who bounded up to join me.

I unpacked the rest of the boxes of books and started processing them into the computer system as well as for the shelves. After that, I figured I might as well get started with getting the event ready. Slightly over two weeks was really not much time at all. I blocked off the date and made a grocery list of things to pick up at the store when the time came.

The library doors opened and my boyfriend, Grayson, came in with a smile for me. My heart gave a little leap when I saw him. His blue eyes lit up when he spotted me. He was handsome but didn't seem to care much about his looks. He was dressed as usual in jeans and a button-down shirt with the sleeves rolled up.

Luna, my coworker, always seemed to know when Grayson had entered the building. It's almost as if she were somehow equipped with radar. She walked up to join us from the children's department, which is where she works.

"Hey, you two," said Luna in a playful voice. "What's up?"

Grayson said, "I hoped *you* knew what was up. I'm actually at loose ends at work because there doesn't appear to be that much to write up."

Grayson was the editor of the local newspaper. He covered everything from hard news (which there was usually very little) to 100th birthday celebrations and everything in between.

Luna nodded. "I had a feeling there might be a dry spell for you in terms of news. It's been very quiet around town lately. No festivals, no events, nothing much going on."

"Which can be a good thing," I reminded them, "except in terms of newspaper reporting. It's good you showed up, though, Grayson. I have something for you. In fact, I was going to give you a call as soon as I started with promo."

Luna's wide eyes grew even wider. "Here? There's something going on *here*? How did I miss that? When did that happen?"

"I think you were busy shelving. Anyway, have either of you read this book?" I picked it up from the desk and held it up. The cover design was fairly unique with the one-word title, *Guilty*, coming out of the fog.

Luna shook her head. "I've heard about it, though. It's on my to-be-read list."

Grayson said, "I bought it. The reviews said it was 'wretched and enthralling' or something like that. Those were a couple of adjectives that rarely go together, and it interested me enough to want to check it out."

I turned the cover around and showed the back to Luna. There was a photo of Sally in a black dress, looking somewhat uncomfortable at having her picture taken. In the picture, she was attempting to smile, but her expression looked as though she'd just eaten something sour. I couldn't imagine that was the best photo her photographer had captured.

Luna frowned and leaned in to take a closer look. "Hey, is that—well, I don't know her name. Is she the woman who's—" She pointed over to the quiet study area.

I nodded. "In the flesh."

Grayson raised his eyebrows. "She's local? Sally Simmons?"

"The very one. She wrote the book here in the library. From what I gather, anyway. She was here every day with her laptop for ages. Anyway, Wilson wanted her in for an event, so we just set that up with her for a couple of weeks from now."

Luna made a face. "That's not a lot of time for set-up."

"You're right. But you know how Wilson can be when he's excited about something. It's like he wants to do it right then. So that's why I was about to ring you up, Grayson—to help get the word out. Think you can put a story in the newspaper to draw attention to the event?"

"You better believe I will. This qualifies as a huge story, especially considering the fact I don't have anything else right now. The biggest story I had until you told me about this was coverage of the high school's tennis team fundraiser. Even if I *did* have something else, this would still be big. I wonder if I can talk with Sally and get a quote or two for the paper, ahead of the event. What's she like?"

I considered this. "Well, I don't really know her, of course, regardless of the amount of time she's spent here. She's the kind of person who keeps to herself, I think. Sally didn't speak to me at all during the last few months."

"Not even to say good morning?" Luna looked a little indignant on my behalf at this.

I shook my head. "I figured she must have been studying or working on something very important and I didn't want to bother here. When Wilson and I were speaking with her earlier, she couldn't seem to get away fast enough from us. But then, she may be working on a follow-up book and trying to outline or draft it. I haven't read *Guilty* myself, so that's something else I need to do in the next couple of weeks."

"What's the format for the event?" asked Grayson.

"The way Wilson was talking, he wants her to speak first, then there's an audience Q&A afterward. Pretty straightforward. I hope she'll be able to talk for a while. She seemed as if she could be pretty quiet."

Grayson said, "I'll slip back there and see if she has a second to talk with me. Is anyone else in the quiet area?"

I shook my head and watched as Grayson headed to the back corner of the room. As taciturn as Sally had been, I wondered if he was going to be instantly rejected. But then, I supposed reporters were likely used to that.

I was taking pictures of Fitz with Sally's book, when Grayson came back over.

"You must have had some luck," I said.

He grinned at me. "You sound surprised."

"I just didn't get the impression that Sally was very excited about the event. I mean, she was interested in doing it, but she wasn't exactly turning cartwheels."

Grayson said, "She was definitely freezing me out until she realized I was with the newspaper and wanted to write an article to promote the event."

"At least she's wanting people there. That's promising."

"Since her book is a bestseller, I'm guessing she's had plenty of interviews and appearances," said Grayson.

"I'll check online," I said. "I know it's only been a few weeks since the book's been out. But I feel like I'd have caught on faster that she was a bestseller if she'd done a lot of interviews and events."

Fitz, released from his duty as a book model, bumped his head against Grayson's hand and Grayson absently scratched him under his chin. Then Fitz flopped on his back, asking Grayson to rub his tummy.

Grayson chuckled. "Now, that's a sweet cat. I remember the tabby cat my parents had when I was growing up. It would have taken my hand off if I'd tried rubbing his belly."

"Fitz is practically a therapy cat," I said. "He makes people smile every day."

I searched for Sally's name online. The book itself came up a ton of times, in all formats and all sorts of retail sites. After a bit more searching, I said, "Well, I see she's written a few blog posts for different websites, and there have been a couple of online interviews, but no videos. She doesn't seem to have much of a presence on social media, either."

"Do writers usually have a big profile?"

I looked up from my computer. "From what I understand, publishers like their authors to have a good-sized following online. In fact, they usually prefer to sign writers who already have a platform set up. I guess her book must have really blown them away."

"You've got it on your reading list now?"

I nodded. "I'm reading *Don Quixote*, but I'm almost done. I'll finish it up tonight so that I can start reading *Guilty*. I don't have any time to waste to read it and come up with questions."

"Was it Wilson's idea to have the author event here?"

I said, "Oh, you know how he is. He likes things done yesterday. But I can definitely pull it together. It's just going to be a busy couple of weeks."

Chapter Two

And, prophetically, I was swamped. During that time, I coordinated the food, the promo, and the taping of the event so that it would be available online to patrons. And, of course, I was doing my usual library work, too. Time flew during those two weeks and before I knew it, it was the day of the author event.

Wilson, thankfully, had extra staff at the library to help. I was busy in the community room, making sure everything was set up. Patrons were already coming in, grabbing a snack and some coffee or soda, and sitting down in chairs to wait for the start of the program. There were also plenty of new faces in the room, which always gave me a lift. I hoped the new folks would start coming into the library regularly and feel comfortable here.

The only thing that made me nervous was the fact that Sally hadn't shown up yet. I always relaxed more at library events when the speaker arrived early. Although I could put this to the back of my mind, I could tell Wilson was very tense. We'd put a good deal of time and a sizeable portion of our event budget into planning this, and it would be awful if Sally didn't show up.

A few minutes later, though, I breathed a sigh of relief when Sally finally entered the community room. She was wearing a plain black dress and black flats and had her blonde hair pulled back tightly in its customary braid. Sally looked nervous and also strangely sullen. Almost defiant. I hoped she would engage with the audience, but her gaze was darting around the room as more people came in.

Wilson had already strolled over to speak with her and, hopefully, get Sally loosened up before the event started. Grayson winked at me from the back of the room, knowing I must be thankful Sally had finally arrived. He'd come early to help me set out chairs for everyone who'd registered to be there. Now he was settled in the back so he could take pictures of the event for the paper.

Wilson led Sally my way, and I smiled at her. "Thanks again for being here. We've got a good-sized group attending today."

Sally's gaze flitted around the room, seeming to rest on a couple of faces from time-to-time. She moistened her lips as if they were dry and said, "Sounds good."

"Did you bring books to sign?"

Sally looked taken aback for a moment and then said, "I forgot."

"That's fine. The signing was completely optional. From what I can see, though, a few people have brought their copies of the books with them, so maybe you can sign those after the event."

Sally shrugged. "I suppose so."

"Perfect," I said, as if Sally had given a more enthusiastic reply. "So here's the way it's going to run Wilson will say a few words to introduce you, then we'll give you the opportunity to speak for fifteen minutes or so. Then I'll ask the questions about the book. You saw my email and got the questions in advance?"

I had to ask because Sally didn't respond to my email. I'd figured she was probably too busy to do so.

She nodded and then thanked me reluctantly, as if the words had been pulled out of her.

I smiled at her. "You must be thrilled your book is on the bestseller list. Did you know it was going to resonate so much with readers?"

Sally shrugged, her gaze dancing around the room again. "I didn't really think about it. I wrote what I wanted to write. I guess it's the kind of story readers went for. I mean, I'm glad about that, of course."

"I've noticed you've still been coming to the library every day. Are you perhaps working on another book?"

Sally turned her brooding eyes back toward me. "Yes. It's actually going to be a sequel."

"That's great! Maybe you can announce that here and that way readers will be on the lookout for it when the book releases."

"That's not a bad idea," said Sally. Then she turned and headed for the chair at the front of the room near the lectern I'd set up.

I wasn't sure Sally was too keen on being there, but the patrons seemed to be having a good time, at least. Many of them seemed to be acquainted with each other, which was often the case in Whitby. The room was full of laughter and people catching up with each other over food.

A few minutes later, Wilson started the program and introduced Sally. He was always a skilled speaker, and his introduction was glowing. Sally looked down at her black dress and seemed to pull at a loose thread on the garment as he spoke. I wondered if it could be nerves that was making her act the way she was.

I had a few nerves myself, hoping Sally would make a decent speaker and that the program wouldn't be over in fifteen minutes. If she gave one-or two-word answers to my questions, things could run really short.

But my fears were alleviated when she moved to the lectern to speak. Sally turned out to be a good speaker. She smoothly talked about how long she wanted to be a writer, the types of classes she'd taken in school, and the sorts of books she enjoyed reading. This was all good information for the library crowd, and they listened to her with interest.

From my position at the front of the room, I noticed there seemed to be at least a couple of people in the audience in the back of the room who didn't appear to be enjoying themselves as much as some of the others. They were riveted to what Sally was saying, but their eyes were narrowed, and they looked tense. I wondered if they could possibly be jealous of Sally's success as a local-girl-made-good or if there was some other reason they were looking that way. Surely, they wouldn't have attended the event if they weren't interested or didn't like Sally.

I focused back in on Sally, who seemed to be hitting her stride.

She smiled at the room and said in her clear, high voice, "One of the things I think readers responded to in my book was the study of guilt. You know, guilt really can rule our lives, can't it?'

The members of the audience looked interested but dubious, so Sally continued. "Think about it. We always talk about guilt trips, but have we really thought about how much it controls how we behave? It's a powerful emotion. It can affect where we spend our holidays, for instance. Which side of the family are you getting the biggest guilt trips from? That's probably going to influence who you're spending Christmas with."

Now the audience members were nodding their heads ruefully.

Sally said, "And, in the case of my novel, guilt can have even greater consequences. That's why I named the novel *Guilty*."

I saw Grayson standing up at the back and taking a few pictures of Sally at the lectern, turning his camera back and forth.

Sally went on to talk about her writing routine and pleased Wilson by dropping a mention of the library and the fact it was her primary place to work.

After Sally wrapped up, I stood with my list of questions. After I quickly introduced myself, we jumped right into it.

"Could you tell us a little about your inspiration for the novel?" I asked with a smile. "Were any elements inspired by actual current events or crime stories? Or were they all completely fictional?"

Sally gave a small smile and said, "The seed of inspiration came from real events, yes. Although of course I fictionalized the book."

I sensed movement coming from the back of the room but wasn't sure what was making people restless. I quickly glanced at my watch to make sure we were on track with the time, but we were actually running ahead of schedule.

"Are you working on anything new?" I asked, although I already knew the answer to that one.

Sally nodded. "I'm working on a follow-up to book one. It's tentatively titled *Risk*."

"Another novel?"

Sally said, "I'm going to be working on nonfiction this time. Southern crime."

There was a murmur from the audience that sounded like excitement to me. I asked four or five more questions, and then the audience Q&A started. There were a few thoughtful questions from patrons who'd clearly already read the book, and then some more general questions. Sally handled it all gracefully, which made me very relieved.

After the session wrapped up, I directed the guests who'd brought books over to the table for them to be signed. I put a couple of pens in front of Sally. Unfortunately, the sullenness seemed about to descend on her again, and she again seemed distracted. Her gaze was focused on the back of the room and not the people she was signing for.

Wilson appeared to be pleased with the program, which was key to how I felt about it. He was smiling and looked upbeat. Grayson, after taking a few more pictures of Sally signing books, gave me a grin and a thumbs-up.

After the event was over and the last patron had left the room, Sally slumped at the table.

I said, "You did a great job up there. You seemed like a really natural speaker. Have you done much public speaking?"

Sally shook her head. "No. I turn down most opportunities to give talks."

"Well, we're glad you accepted this one," I said with a smile.

Sally said, "It's my hometown. I figured maybe I should make the effort." She stood up and gathered her few things. She pulled the homemade scarf from her bag and put it around her neck.

"Pretty scarf," I said.

Sally finally gave me a faint smile. "I made it. It was my hobby before I took up writing."

"We were a little worried we kept the temperature in the library too cool for you."

Sally gave a dour smile. "You could set the temperature at 75 and I'd still be chilly. That's the way I am. I never have been able to really warm up." She picked up her bag, spoke with Wilson for a few minutes, and headed quickly away.

Grayson stuck around to give me a hand putting the room back together. He folded up chairs while I took care of the trash and put away the lectern.

"You had a nice crowd here," he said. "I saw Wilson smiling."

"That's the true sign of a successful program," I said with a chuckle. "Wilson is definitely the gauge of that."

"It almost seemed like Sally was enjoying herself. Unless she's an excellent actress."

I said, "Did you think so? It looked like she's totally wiped out now, so I wondered if she was having to put on a public persona. I'd think it would be exhausting having to keep up a façade for that long."

"I'd wondered at first if she was going to be able to rise to the occasion. She seems like a real introvert. But then, I guess you are, too, aren't you?"

I grinned at him. "The kind of introvert who chose to work around books all day. But I work with *people* all day, too. The payoff is the fact that I enjoy helping patrons out."

Grayson finished with the chairs and then looked at the digital display on his camera. "I think I got some good shots of her." He showed me the camera, and I nodded. He continued, "I'll run a couple of these in the paper tomorrow with a write-up. Do you want me to mention a couple of future upcoming events here? Or just refer readers to the library calendar site?"

I considered this for a moment. "Maybe to the site. Thanks, Grayson."

We chatted for a few more minutes before Grayson had to head back to the newspaper office.

I was turning the lights off in the community room when Wilson walked up. "Great job, Ann," he said, beaming. "The program went off without a hitch. And we had a great number of attendees. Your promo was obviously excellent, as usual."

I motioned over to Fitz, who I could see was on the reference desk, waiting for me. "Fitz was a very cooperative model. I ran a few different things on social media and the content got great engagement."

"Shares and likes, then?" Wilson was always a little bemused at the inner workings of social media since he wasn't on it himself. But he knew the basics.

"Exactly. I recognized some new faces in the audience, so maybe they'll feel comfortable coming back and joining us again."

Wilson nodded. He said, "I saw Sally step outside the building for a few minutes, but then she came back and headed to the quiet area."

I said, "She's one who likes to keep to a routine. She probably decided it would be better if she went ahead and stuck around and knocked her work out while she was here."

Wilson hurried off to his office at the sound of a ringing phone, and I settled back down at the reference desk with Fitz. He was in a particularly affectionate mood and settled himself in my lap as I worked on the computer.

A couple of hours went quickly by. Patrons came up to ask questions, find materials, and hand me books to re-shelve.

I saw someone hurrying up to me out of the corner of my eye and smiled at Linus Truman. He was one of my favorite patrons. An elderly man, he was wearing his suit minus the jacket, as usual. But then I frowned. Linus wasn't looking particularly well. His face was a grayish-green color.

"Is everything all right, Linus? Aren't you feeling well?"

He shook his head solemnly. "Ann, we need to call the police."

Now I was really alarmed. "The police? Why? What's happened?"

"Sally Simmons is dead."

Chapter Three

I gaped at Linus, unwilling to believe the words he was saying. But at the same time, I believed every word. "Oh no. Are you sure?"

He nodded, lips pressed together. "I checked."

Linus definitely wasn't looking well. I said, "Here, have a seat." I motioned him around the desk to my chair. I stood and hurried over to Wilson's office to let him know while calling Burton Edison, the police chief. He picked the phone up right away.

"Ann?" asked Burton. "Everything okay?"

"Sally Simmons is dead here in the library," I said, my mouth dry. "One of our patrons, Linus, found her."

"I'll be right there," said Burton grimly.

Wilson heard me as I stood in his office doorway. He was grimly shaking his head, clearly not wanting to believe what I was saying. I understood how he felt. Since she'd written her book here at the library, Sally felt like one of our own. We'd just had a successful event. Now our speaker was dead? What's more, she was a well-known figure. And it happened here.

I quickly filled in Wilson. He made an announcement on the intercom saying there'd been an incident and he needed everyone to exit the library calmly, but to remain on the property for the time being.

Fortunately, we had plenty of extra staff on hand because of the program. They were directing patrons out the door, and I spotted Linus following them. I headed over to the quiet area to see Sally for myself.

Careful not to touch anything, I got within a couple of yards and realized Linus was indeed correct—Sally was decidedly dead. She'd been strangled with her cheerful homemade scarf, and her body was distorted at the small desk where she was working. I felt genuine sadness as I stepped away and headed outside with everyone else. Again I filled Wilson in. He listened with a horrified expression on his face.

Burton was there quickly and asked Wilson and me to ensure no one left the premises. We told him where to go to find Sally.

Wilson's face was pale. "How could this have happened?"

It seemed like a rhetorical question, so I just nodded to show I understood.

"Was anyone else working back there? In the quiet area, I mean?" asked Wilson.

I said, "I was wondering the same thing. Unfortunately, that area is completely out of eyesight, as you know. We have that mirror back there, but I didn't check it. I don't know who was back there with Sally."

"Were you the one who found her?" asked Wilson. He was clearly hoping none of the patrons had stumbled across Sally.

I shook my head. "I'm afraid it was Linus Truman." Then I frowned, glancing around the group of people assembled in the parking lot. "Where *is* Linus?"

Now Wilson looked even more anxious. "Don't tell me something happened to *him*."

I turned and looked behind us. Sure enough, Linus was sitting apart from the crowd on the curb. He carefully brushed himself off and came over, looking pale.

Wilson said, "We're so sorry you had to go through this. What a terrible thing to happen."

Linus gave him a solemn nod. "Awful."

Wilson looked as if he were going to ask him something, but then he stopped as the library doors opened, and a solemn Burton came out.

While Burton was on the steps of the library, he asked for everyone's attention. In a clear voice, he asked that everyone stay put to give statements and apologized in advance for the time it would take. He said that the state police were on the way and would assist him. Then he headed over to us.

He said to Linus, "I believe you might have discovered the victim, sir, is that correct?" Burton had been introduced to Linus during the days he'd been dating Luna.

Linus pushed his glasses up his nose and nodded. "I'm afraid so."

Linus gave Burton his full name and address. Then Burton asked, "I believe that section of the library is the quiet area, isn't it?"

We all nodded. Burton said, "I remember that you're a regular at the library. Is that ordinarily the section you're sitting in?"

Linus shook his head, taking a deep breath. "I usually spend much of my day in the periodicals section. That way I can catch up on the newspapers, read magazines, and then spend the rest of the time reading my book in a more-comfortable armchair.

The chairs in the quiet area are more functional than comfortable."

I could tell Linus was nervous from his lengthy response. He was not usually much of a talker. I gave him a reassuring smile.

Burton nodded. "Do you have a view from the periodicals section of the quiet area?" When he saw Linus hesitate, Burton elaborated, "Were you able to see anyone approach the area? Or the victim?"

Linus slowly said, "I'm afraid not. The only reason I noticed what had happened is because I was looking for a particular book. The quiet area was in view of those shelves. I glanced over and saw Sally Simmons there, slumped over. I didn't touch her, but I could tell she was . . . no longer living."

"And you knew Ms. Simmons?" asked Burton.

Linus looked confused and Burton said, "You knew who she was, so I just assumed the two of you knew each other."

Linus cleared his throat. "I'm afraid not. The only reason I knew who she was is because I've read her book, *Guilty*. And, of course, I've seen her around the library for quite a few months. She and I had a similar daily routine here. We arrive at about the same time, leave for lunch around the same time . . . that sort of thing."

"But you'd never spoken to her?"

"I'm afraid not," Linus answered once again.

Burton gave him a smile. "Well, I'm sorry you had to find her. That must be very upsetting. You're free to leave the library now; if I have more questions, I'll give you a call."

Linus headed away, looking relieved.

"I don't suppose Linus had anything to do with this?" Burton asked Wilson and me in a low voice. "You're not aware of any connections between the two of them?"

"None at all," I said stoutly. "I never saw them speak with each other. But Linus generally keeps to himself, and so did Sally."

Wilson was looking restless, so Burton focused on asking him questions first. But it was quickly obvious that Wilson had been in his office on the phone and hadn't seen or noticed anything at all. As soon as Burton finished asking him questions, Wilson hurried away to mingle with the patrons and apologize for their having to stay put.

More police drove up then and Burton spoke with them for a few minutes before directing his attention to me. "I couldn't help but notice when I was inside that there were posters of the victim's face all over the library. She was there earlier for a program?"

I nodded. "Sally gave a talk and had a signing today in the community room. She said she was working on a follow-up book, which is apparently why she was working in the library afterward. Linus is right—she's definitely one to keep to a schedule. As far as I've been able to tell, she rigidly adhered to it."

"How did Sally appear during the talk? Did she seem concerned about anything at all? Could her assailant have possibly attended her talk?"

I said, "Well, I was worried to start out with because Sally seemed sort of moody. Quiet. I wasn't sure if she was going to be chatty enough to carry off a lecture and a Q&A session. But then she loosened up as soon as she started. She was animated and seemed to enjoy herself."

"And the audience?"

I said, "They were paying close attention. Sally was a good speaker, and they were definitely onboard." I paused. "I did notice that Sally seemed almost to be looking for someone when she arrived."

"Looking for someone?" Burton's voice was hopeful.

"That's right. Sally arrived fairly late, which had worried me at first. I wondered if she was going to end up being a no-show. I had the feeling that she was looking for someone in particular when she was scanning the faces in the room. And, when she was speaking, she seemed almost to be directing her points to people in the back."

"Do you remember who was sitting back there?"

I shook my head regretfully. "Sorry, no. I was paying more attention to making sure everything was running on time. I realized we had a good turnout, that there were regular patrons as well as newcomers there, and that Wilson seemed happy with the event. That was more of my focus."

"Was the event filmed? Photographed?" Here Burton looked hopeful again.

"It was, yes. Both. Of course, the focus was on Sally, unfortunately. I had the camera zoomed in fairly close."

Burton's face fell.

"But I kept it running after the event wrapped up for a while. You might be able to see who was in attendance."

Burton nodded. "I'm going to need to get that video, I'm afraid."

"Of course." The film was going to be a problem anyway since we clearly would not be able to air it as we'd previously intended. Not with our speaker murdered so soon after the program ended.

"What did you make of Sally?" asked Burton.

I sighed. "Well, I didn't really know her, of course, so it's a little unfair of me to say this. But she wasn't very likeable, I'm afraid. Or, at least, *I* didn't find her very likeable. She seemed to have something of a sour disposition. She didn't interact with the staff."

"Not even with Luna?" Burton gave a wry smile. He'd dated Luna for a time and knew well how extroverted she was. She'd even pulled Linus out of his shell before he'd become so friendly with us.

"Not even with Luna. As far as I'm aware, of course. You'll have to ask her. She's trying to help the moms corral their kids since the children's section is her area."

Burton said, "I know we'll get the video of the event and are going to be scrutinizing it from every direction. But what was your impression of Sally's talk? Did she go off in any directions that were surprising to you?"

I considered this. "I would have said it was basically a normal author talk. She spoke about her background, her interest in writing, and that sort of thing. Pretty normal stuff." I paused. "I would say she did talk about the premise of her book for a little longer than usual. Authors ordinarily like to tease the audience more about the book to tempt them into buying it. But she basically laid it all out for them."

"I'm sure I'm going to start reading her book today. But could you give me a preview?"

I said, "It's a study on guilt."

Burton's eyebrows raised. "Is it now? And you say she was looking for someone in the audience?"

"She seemed to be, yes. But Burton, the book is supposed to be fiction."

Burton said, "Maybe it's based on real-life, though."

"She did say she was starting a new book. And that one was to be nonfiction about a Southern murder."

Burton's eyebrows now raised even higher. "Is that so? I'll have to take a look at that manuscript."

"Her laptop is in the library with her," I said. I felt a sudden wave of sadness thinking of Sally in her homemade scarf.

We were interrupted by a rather nondescript young man. He was tall with stooped shoulders and brownish-blond hair. I felt as if I recognized him from the library but didn't think I'd ever spoken with him.

"Can I help you?" asked Burton, a bit brusquely.

"What's going on here?" asked the man. He gestured around him to the police tape, the people standing outside, and the general tension in the air.

"We've had an incident in the library," said Burton, still sounding short.

The man frowned. "Okay. What kind of incident?"

Suddenly, I realized I could place the young man. I'd seen him speaking with Sally at the library on more than one occasion. I said quietly to Burton, "I think this gentleman might know Sally."

Burton's demeanor changed immediately. "You know Sally Simmons?"

The man's expression was irritated, as if everyone should know that. "That's right. She's my sister. I'm Steve Simmons."

Burton glanced around. "Do you want to have a seat so that we can have a talk? My police car is right there."

He shook his head impatiently. "No, I really just want to know what's going on. I don't have time for this. I've got to get back to my job. I'm on a break from the grocery store."

Burton said slowly, "I'm afraid I have some bad news for you. Your sister was discovered, dead, at the library. I'm very sorry."

Steve shook his head again. "That can't be right. There must be some sort of mistake. I just spoke to Sally."

"When was that?" asked Burton, taking out a tiny notebook and a stub of a pencil.

Steve rubbed his face, thinking. "I don't know. Maybe it was an hour ago."

Burton quirked an eyebrow. "And you decided to come over to the library to see her, even though you just talked?"

Steve seemed a little flustered. "There was something I needed to ask her."

"But not on the phone?"

Steve shrugged. "Sally wanted to get back to work. She ended the conversation too fast. Sometimes she could be laser-focused like that. So I just thought I'd pop by the library before I went to work."

"And interrupt her?"

Steve's shrug now was impatient, as if he was trying to deflect Burton's words. "I needed to talk to her, like I said. Anyway, why would I be here now if I'd done something to Sally? I didn't know anything about this. I was at home before now, getting ready to go to work."

Burton continued pressing, after jotting down a note about Steve's previous whereabouts. "Unfortunately, your sister's death is suspicious. There are some routine questions I need to ask. What was so urgent that you needed to speak with your sister about it right then?"

Steve's stooped shoulders fell even more as he gave in. "Suspicious??"

"I'm afraid so."

Steve blew out a shaky breath. "Okay. I needed to ask Sally for a small loan to cover me until payday. My car needed to go to the shop, and I had to use my rent money for that. I wanted to ask her to make up the difference."

"And Sally would have done that?"

Steve said, "She didn't have a problem with that. Sally came into a lot of money recently." He gestured to me. "She'll know. Sally was giving a talk at the library today."

"You couldn't make the talk?" asked Burton.

I noticed a flash of irritation in Steve's eyes. "It's not my kind of thing. Besides, it looked like there were going to be tons of people there. I probably couldn't have found a seat. Besides, I had to get ready to go to work."

"So Sally was doing well with her books," said Burton. "Well enough to help you out, too."

"It's not like she minded. Sally knew she had lots more advantages than I did growing up. I had to drop out of college because my folks ran out of money helping Sally with her education. They thought Sally had more promise than I did, so I guess they had to plan their investment." This was said in a sneering voice.

"What kind of work do you do for the grocery store?" asked Burton.

"Whatever they need me to do. I can stock shelves, unload the truck, bag, ring up groceries. Maybe I'd have been in management if I hadn't had to drop out of school, though. I've been thinking about doing something else, anyway. Maybe getting certified as a bartender and working at Quittin' Time."

Steve had something of a defensive air when he talked about his job.

"What do you know about your sister's book?"

Steve frowned. "What do you mean, what do I know?"

"Have you read it?"

Steve made a face. "It's not really my thing, like I said before. All I know is that the book was based on something that actually happened."

Burton glanced at me. "I understood it was fiction."

Steve shrugged again. "Maybe she said that just so she wouldn't get sued or something. Or maybe somebody gave her the idea for the book. I don't know." He came to an abrupt stop, probably not wanting to suggest that his sister's book wasn't actually her own work.

Burton made some more scribbles in his notepad. "How was Sally lately?"

"How was she?"

Now Burton was the one who sounded a little impatient. I couldn't blame him. It wasn't easy pulling information out of Steve. "Did your sister seem to have something on her mind? Worried about something? That kind of thing."

Steve considered this. "Well, I wouldn't say she was *worried* about anything. She just got this huge windfall of money, you know? She was excited about that, and she was happy that the book had come out and was doing so well. The publisher had given her this big advance, and she wanted to prove to them that the book would sell. And it did." He thought some more. "Sally did just break up with her boyfriend, of course."

Chapter Four

Burton poised the stub of a pencil over the notepad. "What's his name?"

"Jason Hill. They were together for a while, but then Sally dumped him when things started getting crazy for her. I guess she didn't have time for a relationship while she was working on the second book and doing interviews and stuff."

Steve was sort of vague about the details of what Sally was actually up to. And, as I'd noticed earlier, Sally hadn't actually done a lot of press for her book.

"How did Jason take the breakup?" asked Burton.

"Not great," admitted Steve. "I think it made it look like she was using him. But that wasn't Sally, you know."

"Using him? Was he supporting Sally or something?"

Steve nodded. "That's right. She was living with him, and he was helping her out while she was spending her days here." He gestured at the library.

"So *was* Sally using him?" Burton tapped the pencil on the paper.

"No, of course not. Sally would never do something like that. She wanted the relationship to work out. She was always saying how smart Jason was and how he could do anything."

Burton continued tapping the pencil on the notepad thoughtfully. "This Jason—he's a farmer, isn't he?"

"Yeah. He does all right with a kind of small farm. He's got that farm stand where he sells free-range eggs, honey, stuff like that. I'm not sure Sally really pictured herself as a farmer's wife, though. Jason thought they were a lot more serious than she did."

"Was he mad about the breakup?" asked Burton.

"You'll have to ask him that. But the impression I got from Sally was that he was furious. Nobody likes to feel like they've been used. And maybe Sally didn't do the best job explaining why she was breaking up with him. That's the thing about Sally—she was good with words when she was writing. But when she was talking, she got real awkward."

"Anything else you can tell me about your sister that might help us figure out who did this? What kind of person she was, what her interests were?" asked Burton.

Steve was quiet for a few seconds. "I don't know, really. I mean, she was pretty quiet. She didn't have many friends. That's why I was glad she was dating Jason. I didn't like the thought of her being by herself all the time."

"Was it usual for her not to have friends, or did she fall out with some people recently?"

Steve said, "It was pretty normal, unfortunately. Like I said, she could be really awkward. And she mostly enjoyed doing quiet activities, anyway. She'd go on walks, read books, listen to music. Sally didn't spend a lot of time out of the house."

"What did she do before she started writing books? She had some income before then?"

Steve said, "Sally worked in an office for a while. It was the front office for one of the mills around here. I don't know exactly what she did for them, but I don't think she liked it much. She told me that she had to write that book she was working on. She was driven."

Burton said, "Is there anyone else you can think of who might have had a problem with Sally?"

"With Sally?" Steve sounded surprised.

"You can't think of anyone other than the ex-boyfriend?"

Steve opened his mouth and then closed it again. "At first, I was going to reject the idea that anybody could have wanted to hurt Sally. Like I said, she kept to herself. How could you make someone upset if you just hang out in the library or at home? But there was this one woman that Sally was having issues with. She told me about it recently."

Burton's pencil was poised over the notepad. "Do you know her name?"

"It was Liz . . . no, *Liv*. That was it. I don't know much about it because Sally didn't mention it more than once or twice. But this Liv started bugging Sally right after the book came out and got big."

I knew a Liv from the library and had a feeling it must be the same one Steve was referring to. There couldn't be more than one in a town the size of Whitby.

Burton asked, "Bugging her? Like how?"

"Oh, I don't know. Calling her, I guess? Sending her emails? Anyway, she was being a pest for Sally to say something about it to me. That's all I know, though."

Burton nodded, making another few notes. He also asked for Steve's contact information. "Okay. Steve, I'm sorry again about your sister. We're going to do everything we can to figure out who's responsible for this."

Steve nodded and moved slowly toward his car, lost in his own thoughts once again.

Burton glanced across at the crowd of people. "I'd better check in again with the other cops. See you later, Ann."

He moved away to speak with the forensics team, who had just arrived on the scene.

Luna hurried toward me. "What a mess. I can't believe this is happening at the library again. This is my safe place."

I nodded, knowing exactly how she felt. "I know. It feels like a violation, doesn't it? I guess we shouldn't be too shocked. After all, it's a public place and whatever happens in the public can happen there. But it just feels wrong." I looked around the crowd of patrons. "Wow, all the moms and kids are gone."

Luna gave a small smile. "Yeah. I told the state police they needed to get the kids out of there first thing. Of course, we were in the middle of a storytime when we got the announcement to leave the building. I grabbed a few picture books on the way out and read stories while the cops talked to the moms and got their witness statements."

"That must have been pretty quick."

Luna shrugged. "They wouldn't have seen anything unless it happened before they were in storytime. Sally's death took place completely across the building. And after all, no mom in her right mind is going to take little kids over to the quiet area of the library."

"No, I guess not."

Luna said, "What on earth happened? I mean, I *know* what happened, but I can't figure out why it did. We had a perfectly nice event from everything I've heard. Then our speaker ends up dead shortly afterward?"

I nodded slowly. "I get the feeling that it must have had something to do with what was said at the program. I've read the book now, of course, and Sally swore it was fiction. I'm wondering how much of it might have been based on real events, though. Plus, Sally said that she was working on a second book now that was nonfiction. On some sort of Southern murder or murders. Maybe someone wanted to stop her from doing that."

"Did you notice anybody acting weird during the program? Glaring at Sally or something?"

"Not really," I said. "There were a lot of people there—the room was packed. I was mostly focused on Sally and thinking about the questions I was going to ask her following the session. She'd answered some of them during her talk, so I was striking those out. Plus, everyone in the room looked pretty serious. Sally was a good speaker, but she wasn't throwing a lot of jokes in there. Her book wasn't exactly a light-hearted read, either."

"Uh-oh," muttered Luna. "Don't look now, but Zelda's on her way over."

I groaned. A little Zelda went a long way with me. Not only was she my neighbor and homeowner association president, but she was also a regular volunteer at the library. I was getting double doses of Zelda, which could be hard to handle. I kept telling myself that she meant well, although she could be abrasive.

Zelda was indeed striding over in our direction, and she looked cranky. There was a cigarette in her hand, which she certainly didn't need. Her grating voice was already ruined from a lifetime of smoking. Her henna-colored hair was fairly bristling with indignation as she approached.

"What's going on here?" she asked, waving her cigarette around to indicate the police, the emergency vehicles, and the patrons and staff milling around in the parking lot.

Luna said sadly, "Our speaker died."

"What?" demanded Zelda. "During the library program?" Her voice indicated that she thought our speaker had very poor taste.

I shook my head. "Afterward. It looks like a suspicious death."

The death wasn't the only suspicious thing. Zelda's eyes were full of it. "Somebody did our speaker in?"

Luna and I nodded. "That's what it looks like," I said.

Zelda's brow was furrowed. "That's the young woman who would type in the quiet area."

Of course, Zelda would know who she was. She spent a lot of time shelving in the various nooks and crannies of the building.

"Did you read her book?" asked Luna.

I winced on Luna's behalf.

Zelda glared at Luna. "Of course not!" she hissed. "I don't read books. No time for that nonsense."

Luna didn't seem to be able to tell when she needed to quit. "Did you make it to the event?"

"No, I didn't. I'm not at the library to *enjoy* myself. I'm here to volunteer."

This made it sound as if volunteering were sheer torture that she reluctantly endured.

Speaking of volunteering made Zelda return to her original train of thought. "When is all of this going to be finished with? I have shelving to do."

"Definitely not today. We'll be closing the rest of the day out of respect for Sally. Plus, the police and forensics need to spend time in the building to investigate," I said.

Zelda blew out an annoyed sigh, as if murder were quite an inconvenience.

I said, "Did you ever meet or speak with Sally? I know you spend some time back in that section of the library when you're volunteering."

Zelda was already shaking her head halfway through my words. "Nope. But I had my opinions about her."

That sounded likely. Zelda was the sort to form opinions without even speaking with someone.

"What did you think of her?" asked Luna.

"I thought she typed far too loudly," said Zelda. "It's supposed to be a *quiet* area. There are always lots of people in there studying and reading materials. Then there she was, pounding the keys on her keyboard as hard as she possibly could. Very annoying." She pursed her lips. "I guess if I can't volunteer, I'll head over to work. Got to keep busy."

With that, she spun on her heel and stomped off.

Luna said, "She's always very dramatic, isn't she?" Her eyes opened wide. "Hey, I just remembered you were going to tape the program to have folks tune in online. Does Burton know about that?"

I nodded. "I'm going to send him a link to it as soon as I get back home. I'm not sure he's going to be able to tell a lot from it because the camera was mostly focused on Sally, but maybe he'll get a few clues from the questions the audience asked." I saw a figure hurrying toward me and smiled. "Grayson's here."

We turned and greeted him, and he gave us both a hug. "How are you two doing?"

Luna made a face. "Ann and I were talking about how we don't like things like this happening in our safe places."

"No," said Grayson, looking grim. "I totally understand that. Are you both free to go? Or does Wilson want you sticking around until all the patrons are allowed to leave?"

"I'll ask him," said Luna, walking off toward Wilson, who was now standing by himself and watching the police come and go from the building.

Grayson gave me a searching look, as if trying to pick up on my stress level. "I couldn't believe it when I heard it over the police scanner. I mean, the event pulled off without a hitch. Sally was a great speaker. And then she's murdered right afterward?" He shook his head.

"I know. That's the worst. She had a successful talk, and I could tell she felt good about it. Then she headed off to her usual spot to get some work done, and this happens?"

Grayson said, "Did you think it was sort of odd for her to be going right back to work after her program?"

"Not really. I mean, *I* wouldn't have wanted to. Sally seemed like she was a real introvert, and I'd think she'd have been exhausted after being in the public eye for a couple of hours. But I know how routine-driven she was. I think she wanted to stay on-track with her story and keep her routine in order."

Luna came back over to us. "Wilson said he didn't need us to stick around. He didn't see any reason for us to. He's going to have Burton call him and let him know when the police are wrapping up so that he can come back later and lock up."

I looked over at Wilson and sighed. "Looks like maybe Wilson has momentarily changed his mind. He's bringing a patron over here."

Grayson said, "I'll be right back. It looks like Burton has a free moment and I was going to see if I could get a quote for the paper from him."

Wilson walked up with a young man in tow. I recognized him as Jason Hill, who had the roadside stand with all sorts of produce. Jason was tall and always had a rather old-fashioned look about him.

Wilson, always very proper, introduced the two of us, regardless.

Jason bobbed his head at me and solemnly said, "Hi Ann. I've seen you at the stand, I think."

Wilson said, "Ann, Jason was just telling me that he was over at the library to see Sally. They had a relationship."

I remembered Sally's brother saying that Jason was Sally's *ex*-boyfriend.

Chapter Five

"I'm so sorry about Sally," I said immediately.

Luna quickly echoed my words.

The shock I'd seen on Jason's features turned to sadness. He nodded, wordlessly.

Wilson continued, "Jason wanted to hear more about Sally's morning here. I gave him my impressions, but I thought I'd have you speak with him for a few moments, Ann. Luna wasn't actually at the program because she was working in the children's section."

Jason said to me, "I just can't believe what happened. Can you help fill me in? It's hard for me to wrap my head around it."

Wilson excused himself and asked Luna if he could speak with her for a minute. They walked away.

I cleared my throat. "Sally was here at the library for a while today, as you probably know."

Jason nodded. "She had the event today. I couldn't come because there were things I needed to do at the farm. Plus, we really hadn't figured out what our boundaries were, post-breakup." He took a deep breath. "Sally and I broke up weeks ago."

"I'm sorry," I said again.

Jason gave a philosophic wave of his hand. "These things happen. I was sure we were going to end up back together again, by the end." His voice broke at the end, and I waited until he gained control again. "I guess that's not going to happen now. Anyway, that's one reason why I wasn't here today."

"The program went really well," I said. "Sally did a fantastic job with her talk, the Q&A session afterward, and the signing. The audience was very engaged."

Jason looked a little surprised by this. "That's great. I guess I never really thought of Sally as much of a speaker."

"Have you heard her speak before?" This was still on my mind because of what seemed like a lack of engagements.

"No. But just knowing Sally, she's not one for entertaining a group. Or, well, much of anybody."

I asked, "Was she shy?"

"I wouldn't say she was *shy*. Sally was just sort of withdrawn, I guess. Quiet. Reserved. That kind of thing. She didn't have a lot of friends."

That was something else I'd been wondering. It would be tricky for Burton to get a feel for Sally without having friends or family for him to talk with. I wasn't sure what kind of impression he was going to be able to get from speaking with an ex-boyfriend, her brother, and the library staff.

Burton must have been a mind-reader because when I glanced up, he was looking right at me from across the parking lot. He gave me a questioning look, and I motioned him over.

"Sorry, but I think Burton Edison is going to want to speak with you," I said.

Jason frowned. "The police chief." Now he looked uneasy. "He's not going to think I'm a suspect, is he? I mean, with the breakup and all. Sally and I were on good terms."

"I'm thinking he's going to want to talk with anybody who knew Sally," I said. "He probably wants to paint a picture of who she was."

Burton joined us, his notepad out again. "Hi, there. Jason, isn't it? I've run by your farm stand quite a few times during apple season. I like those honeycrisp apples you've got over there."

Burton was excellent at putting people at ease. I saw Jason relax a bit at the friendly approach.

"Honeycrisps are real popular," he said. "Everybody likes that sweet taste."

Burton nodded. "The nice thing about your stand is you don't charge more for them. At the stand on the other side of town, he charges a dollar extra for that particular variety."

Having complimented Jason on his pricing and his choice of produce, Burton hopped into a few questions. "It looks to me like you might have known Sally Simmons, just judging from how stressed you look right now."

Jason nodded, and Burton told him he was sorry for his loss. Burton continued, "Was she a friend of yours?"

"Girlfriend," offered Jason. Then he edited himself. "Former girlfriend, actually. But we were going to get back together. Sally had just gotten real busy with the book coming out, and she didn't have time for a relationship."

Burton said, "I see. So the relationship was sort of on hold."

Knowing Burton, I could tell he was taking that information with a grain of salt. But Jason took his words at face value and nodded eagerly again.

Burton continued, "Sally's book was the reason you broke up, you say? Or were taking a break?"

"That's right. I mean, before then she was busy, too. She spent a lot of time here," he said, gesturing to the library. "But she always came back home to me. We'd have an early supper and watch TV together. We were always pretty laid back. But then, once she got the book deal, she said she just didn't have time for us." Jason gave a shrug. "I knew she was going to come back, though, just as soon as things settled down some."

Burton scratched his head. "I don't know much about book publishing. What kind of stuff was Sally doing that was taking up so much time?"

Jason looked as if he was at a loss himself. "I know a lot more about farming than publishing."

They looked at me, the librarian in the group, to shed some light. "Ordinarily, the writer would be doing a good amount of promo. There would be social media posts and blog tours. An author might do cover reveals, video interviews, podcasts, and in-person appearances like the one we had today."

"And Sally was doing all of that?" asked Burton.

Jason shrugged again. "I guess so."

But I knew better. Sally had a tiny online footprint. There was no way that she was promoting herself during that time.

Burton tapped his pencil against his notepad. "What did you think of Sally's book?"

Jason put his hands up. "I'm not much of a reader."

"You didn't read it?" asked Burton.

Jason shook his head.

"Did she tell you about it, though? Talk about what was happening in the book?"

Jason considered this. I wondered if he was the type of boyfriend who tuned Sally out when she was talking about her work. He said slowly, "She did, some. But it was mostly that she'd had a good or bad writing day. She'd talk about her word count and where she was in the book. Later on, she'd talk about sending out emails to agents and publishers and that sort of thing." Jason seemed a little vague on the details.

"Nothing about the content of the book?" pushed Burton.

Jason thought again. "I know it was set during college. It had to do with people being involved in a crime and feeling guilty later about it."

Jason gave us both a look that was begging for approval.

Burton gave him an encouraging smile, and I did the same. Burton said, "Did you get the impression Sally was making the story up herself or that it was inspired by actual events?"

Jason now looked worried again, most likely because he didn't know the answer to the question. "I'm not sure. I thought she was making it up. She was spending a lot of time at the library, like I was saying."

Burton, perhaps realizing that asking Jason a lot of questions about the book was futile, said, "How long did the two of you date? And how did you meet each other? Did you go to college together?"

"We dated for years. And we weren't at the same college. I met Sally when she came to the farm stand for free-range eggs."

Which were great, but expensive. When my budget allowed, I'd get some, too. When my budget didn't, as was usually the case, I ended up going to the grocery store.

Burton asked, "Did you live together?"

Jason nodded.

Burton followed this up with, "And was Sally working during the last year or so?"

"On the book, yes."

Burton asked, "But not in a regular job? I mean, did she get money to write the book ahead of time? Like a publishing deal? Or was she writing the book without pay at first?"

"Oh, I see what you're asking. No, she wrote the book first and then started sending it out. Sally wasn't being paid in advance to write the book. And she didn't have a job. Well, she helped me out at the farm stand some days when I needed to irrigate or spray crops so the stand could stay open. But that's about it."

Burton nodded. "Your farm has been around for a while, I think I've heard?"

Jason's expression was proud. "For generations. I'm just glad to keep it going. It meant everything to my dad until the day he wasn't able to keep up with it anymore. He felt like it was easier for him to step away from it knowing somebody in the family was going to continue working it." He paused. "Can you tell me more about what happened here? To Sally? I thought the library was supposed to be a safe place."

I winced a little and was glad Wilson wasn't within earshot.

Burton said evenly, "For the most part, it is. But it's a public space, so that means it's open for people to sort out any differences they have. Right now, there's not much I can disclose about Sally's death except that we are treating it as suspicious."

"She didn't suffer, did she?"

Burton quickly shook his head. "I'm sure she didn't."

That was Burton just being nice. I guessed he thought there was no point in upsetting Jason. Hopefully, her passing had been quick, but I didn't think that was necessarily a fast way to go. I shivered and felt sadness about Sally again.

Jason sighed. "Everything went south as soon as Sally's book got bought by a publisher. That's when everything started—Sally's stress, breaking up with me. Probably even her death was because of that book."

Burton nodded. "Again, I'm very sorry about this. If you think of anything else, let me know." He gave Jason a business card and verified Jason's contact information. Then Jason walked away.

I said, "It sounds like Sally's laptop might have a lot of useful information on it."

"That's true. Especially if she was getting emails from people who weren't happy about the book. Which is now next on my reading list," said Burton grimly. "I'll talk with you later, Ann."

As he took off, I saw Grayson motioning to me across the parking lot. I picked up Fitz, who was likely tiring of being in his carrier, and joined him. He was standing with Luna and his friend, Jeremy, who had recently started hanging out with Luna in a fledgling relationship.

Luna said, "Since we're clearly off today, I was thinking about heading back to my house to see my mom. She heard about what happened here and has been texting me non-stop, even though I've told her I'm fine."

"Once a mom, always a mom," I said with a smile.

Jeremy said, "I was telling Luna that I could run by and play a hand of cards with her before I head back to the office."

That was not only a kind thing for Jeremy to offer, it was also smart. Although Jeremy was very likeable, Mona had definitely had a tough time warming to him. I knew that was because she'd been so fond of Burton, who Luna had dated before Jeremy.

I said, "I could come by, too, after I run Fitz by the house, in case you need another player. Are you going there, too, Grayson?"

He nodded. "Just for a little while. I'll have to head back to the newsroom to write up this story for tomorrow's edition. But I've probably got an hour."

Luna beamed at us. "It's a plan, then. I'll see you over at my house."

I put Fitz in the car with me and drove home. It was good that Fitz was such a laid-back cat. He didn't seem to care at all that he'd been rapidly hustled into his carrier and made to spend an hour in the parking lot with gobs of patrons and emergency workers. He'd just taken it all in stride.

Still, when I let him out of his carrier at home, he trotted right over to his favorite sunbeam and curled up in the little round bed I'd purchased for him. All the stimulation must have tired him out.

All the stimulation tired *me* out, actually, too. Part of me felt like calling Luna and saying I would not make it after all before hitting the sack for a long nap. But I also knew I'd regret that later when it was time to turn in for the night. Instead, I grabbed my keys and headed out the door. Before I locked up, though, I remembered I needed to forward Burton a copy of the video we'd shot in the library that morning. I hurried back over to my laptop bag and pulled out the computer.

It was such a huge file that I realized I couldn't just send it as an attachment to his email. But I also wasn't sure where he would be today while he was out in the field investigating—so it wasn't going to work for me to give him the file on a thumb drive.

Instead, I set up the file online and created a link, which I shared with him. Hopefully that would work. By that time, Fitz had woken up from his nap in the sunbeam. I glanced down at him as he was rubbing against my legs, circling them in the process. "What's up, buddy? Need a little attention?"

I sat down in a chair around the kitchen table, and Fitz jumped nimbly into my lap. I looked at him with a frown. "Uh-oh. You have tufts of fur coming out. Looks like I need to give you a good brushing." I glanced at my watch, hoping I wasn't holding up the card game. Sometimes it was better, though, to knock out tasks when they were on my mind.

Fitz looked resigned as I got the brush out. Getting brushed wasn't his favorite thing in the world. Often, he would treat it like a game, batting at the brush as I went.

I tried to be gentle, pulling the cat brush through his thick fur. He seemed to try, on his end, to help me out by being on his best behavior.

Then he took it a step further, deciding to be even more helpful by grooming himself at the same time. I chuckled as we both worked on his fur.

"There you are," I said finally. "Wow, look how much loose fur I got out. We could build another Fitz with all of that."

He seemed to smile at me, his eyes nearly closing.

"Since you were such a good boy, how about some playtime for a couple of minutes before I have to run?" I pulled out one of his favorite toys from the cabinet. It was the kind of toy that I had to put away to ensure that he didn't end up destroying it whenever I was out running errands. It was a pretty simple cat toy—basically a small fishing line with a "creature" of indeterminate species on the end of it.

Fitz's pupils grew huge as he spotted the toy. He crouched and then batted at the creature over and over again, making its feathery/furry body bob around on the line.

We played for a few minutes until I saw his interest was flagging. I then let the creature fall to the floor. "Looks like you killed him, Fitz."

Fitz looked at the creature, which was lying still on the floor, with satisfaction. He started licking himself, seeming very pleased by his performance.

I gave him a few quick rubs and then left the house.

Chapter Six

Luna lived with her mother, Mona, in the house she'd grown up in. She was allegedly taking care of Mona and giving her a hand around the house, but I'd always had the sneaking suspicion that Mona was helping Luna just as much. The house was a motley assortment of both Mona's well-established tastes and Luna's more colorful style. When I walked in, there was the coziness demonstrated by Mona's crocheted blankets and her quilts. Childhood artwork by Luna still graced the fridge. Luna's contributions were colorful wall hangings in a kaleidoscope of colors and a fair amount of clutter.

Luna, Mona, Jeremy and Grayson were sitting around the dining room table. They greeted her with smiles.

Mona said, "Thank heavens you and Luna are all right, Ann! What a horrible thing to happen. I've been worried sick about you, Luna, and Wilson."

While her mother was turned toward me, Luna made a smiley motion to indicate the current mission was to settle Mona down and be upbeat. I said lightly, "Oh, we're just fine. You know how Luna and I are . . . indestructible."

Luna chimed in. "Librarians have to be. We deal with so many different types of crises over there that we just go with the flow."

Mona said, "Just the same, I'm very relieved."

Grayson said, "We were just about to play hearts."

"Can you even play hearts with five players?" I asked.

"Sure we can. We just have to modify the deck a little. Want me to deal you in?"

"As long as you can give me a quick refresher. Otherwise, I'm going to be the big loser of the group."

Jeremy grinned at me. "Somebody's got to be. Might as well be you."

Which was why I was delighted that I was dealt an excellent hand. I got rid of a couple of hearts and handed my queen of spades to Jeremy, who looked horrified when he saw what I'd passed him. I gave him a wicked grin in return.

Mona proved to not only have an excellent hand, but to be a wily player. She won the first hand.

While Grayson was dealing the cards out again, Luna said to me, "Oh, I almost forgot that I needed to fill you in on what Wilson was talking to me about."

"That sounds ominous," I said with a sigh. "I have the feeling he's wanting to have us embark on yet another program of some kind."

"You nailed it," said Luna. "He noticed when he was talking with the moms outside the library that they seemed pretty unnerved by the happenings today." She gave a quick glance at her mother, but Mona was laughing at something Jeremy had said and wasn't listening in.

"Understandably," I said. "I'm guessing he wanted you to come up with something interesting to bring everyone into the library and make it a fun place again."

"Exactly. But I was thinking—why limit it to the children's department? Because Wilson also asked me to tell you he wanted something similar for the adults. Maybe you and I can col-lude with each other."

"Collusion?" Mona was suddenly listening in again and looking worried. "What's this about Wilson and collusion?"

I quickly said, "We're just trying to think up a library pro-gram that might work just as well for the adults as for the child patrons. With some modifications, of course. You spend a lot of time at the library, Mona—any ideas?"

I'd mostly asked her to get her mind off the murder again, but Mona seemed to take the question quite seriously. She tapped her playing cards on the table as she mulled the question over.

"So a community-building thing, I'm guessing. Wilson would like it if it checked off numerous boxes, of course." Mona chuckled.

Luna grinned at her. "Like if it were green."

"Colored green, dear?"

"No, Mom, I mean if it were eco-friendly."

"I see," said Mona. She smiled. "Then my idea might be truly genius. I read online recently about a seed library."

Jeremy frowned. "People borrow seeds?"

"Well, from what I read, it's more that they *take* them. And they bring seedlings of their own to give away. Maybe you can find out some more information online, Ann—you're so very good at that. But basically, from what I understand, the librari-ans offer seedlings to the community for free. You might get in some very different people, from that program."

I nodded, thinking it over. "The outreach potential sounds really good. And seeds aren't very expensive, which Wilson would appreciate."

Then I looked down at my cards and realized I'd lost the hand. I made a face. "I might as well claim all the rest of the cards. I've got lots of hearts and the queen of spades."

Luna laughed. "Mom distracted you and you lost."

I said ruefully, "I certainly did. Maybe I'll do better on the next hand."

Which I did.

After we'd played hearts, eaten a large snack, courtesy of Mona, and chatted for a while, Grayson and Jeremy both said they needed to head back to work.

After they left, Mona sounded a little fretful again. "I keep thinking about that poor girl. She was in the library, doing her usual thing, and the next thing she knows, it's the end of her life. What a truly terrible thing."

Luna said, "I know. It would have been an even worse feeling if I knew her better than I did. But she never spent much time talking—she was all about getting to work."

Mona nodded. "I'm trying to place her, actually. I know I must have seen her. From what you were saying, she was in the library every day it was open." Then she snapped her fingers. "I think I do remember. Long, blonde hair? A bit of a dour expression?"

"That sounds like Sally," I said.

"She kept to herself, as I recall. Although once, when I dropped my knitting bag, she was kind enough to hand it to me. Aside from that, though, I didn't really have any interaction with her. I remember wondering what had happened to make her look so very unhappy."

I considered this. "Sally seemed unhappy. I thought maybe she was just shy or very introverted. But I think you might be right. She could also have been unhappy."

I glanced at my watch. "I should be heading out, myself. Now that I have an unexpected day off, I need to figure out the best way to spend it."

Luna rolled her eyes. "Don't force yourself to be productive, Ann. You're going to make me look bad."

"Why? What are you planning to do today?"

"Sleep," said Luna. "I've been sleeping really poorly lately and now it's going to be naptime."

"You could read," suggested her mother.

"I could, except the book I'm reading right now is horrid. In fact, it's the exact sort of book that is going to help me fall asleep."

I raised my eyebrows. "That doesn't sound like your usual fare at all. You're usually reading fantasy or science fiction; the kind of stuff that glues you to the pages."

"I know," groaned Luna. "But it's a book Jeremy wanted me to read. It was sweet of him to recommend it. He said it changed his life."

"Really? Maybe *I* need to read it," I said wryly.

Luna shook her head vigorously. "Friends don't let friends read books this boring. It's all full of business-speak mumbo-jumbo and optimizing your life."

"That doesn't really sound like Jeremy's cup of tea," I said.

"Exactly. I guess maybe that's why it was life changing. Except I really hope he doesn't turn into somebody like the author." She sighed. "I'll take another stab at it. It's a pity it doesn't have a synopsis online or something."

Mona asked, "What are you reading right now, Ann?"

"I'm reading *Don Quixote*."

Luna rolled her eyes again. "Now you're just bragging. I love that book. Is it a re-read?"

I shook my head. "It's actually the first time I've read it. Somehow it was never taught to me in school. I'm supposed to lead the book club on it."

After a couple more minutes, I headed away in my old Subaru. I'd meant what I said about having an unexpected day off. The nice thing was that the possibilities were endless. But first, I went back home for a cuddle with Fitz. This somehow led to my very own nap, curled up on the sofa with a very happy, purring kitty.

After carefully removing myself from Fitz, I took the time to make myself a real grocery list. This was the kind of grocery list I didn't ordinarily find the time to make for myself. I took note of what I had in the pantry and the fridge, tossed old food, and then organized the fridge better to make room for the groceries I'd bring home. Then I did some quick meal planning, including lunches since I packed my lunches for work. I pulled some coupons I'd clipped out of the drawer, then headed off to the store.

My phone rang as I pulled into the parking lot. "Burton?" I said, seeing his name appear on my phone.

"Hi. I had a few minutes to review the footage you sent me from the library event. I was wondering if you recognize one particular person. It's someone who was leaving the room after the event had finished."

"So the camera picked up people leaving?"

"And a few who were coming in before the event started, while you were still setting things up," said Burton. "Here, I'm going to text you a screenshot."

I pulled the phone away from my ear and waited a few seconds for a screenshot to appear. When it did, I said, "Yes, I recognize her. That's Liv Nelson. She's in the library a good deal."

Chapter Seven

"This is the same Liv that Steve was talking about? He said she'd been 'bugging' Sally, or something?"

"That's right. At least, that's the only Liv I know in town, so it seems likely."

Burton asked, "Did you ever see her around Sally? Approach her?"

I said slowly, "No, but I wasn't really looking. The quiet section isn't in full view. Like I said, Liv was in the library often, so she could easily have come in one day and headed back to that area to talk with Sally."

"Besides the program, did you notice Liv at the library today?"

I thought about it. "No," I said. "Not to check out any books, at least. But she could easily have been there."

"What do you know about her?"

I said, "She's in her mid-twenties and is a teaching assistant at Whitby College. She's a scholarship student and has always seemed like she takes her studies seriously. That's why she's in the library so often."

"Did she check out Sally's book that you remember?"

I pressed my lips together. Privacy is one of the biggest things we respect at the library. Fortunately, I knew I hadn't checked out the book to her. "Not that I know of."

"Of course, she could have bought it somewhere," said Burton in a distracted voice.

"Definitely. We didn't get the book ourselves until a couple of weeks ago and it had been out for a while."

Someone in the background called out to Burton, and he told them he was coming. "Okay. Thanks for the information. I'm going to try to catch her at home. Or maybe at the college since she's teaching there. Talk to you later."

I finally got out of the car and did my grocery shopping. It was a good thing I had a list because I was pretty distracted during the process. When I got back home, I put the groceries away and started with meal prep. After that, I found it was silent in the house.

Fitz, although a very social animal, was perfectly content with the silence in the house. He looked at me fetchingly from the sofa, inquiring if I wanted to spend more time with *Don Quixote* and him.

Instead, I texted Grayson to see if he wanted to come over and hang out with Fitz and me. He called me back instead of texting.

"Hi there," he said, a smile in his voice. "Feeling at loose ends?"

"I am. And it's an unusual feeling for me. Are you free at all? I was wondering if you'd like to kill time."

Grayson now sounded rueful. "I'd love to, but I'm totally swamped. I started out writing the story for the paper tomorrow. Then we ended up with a score of tech issues at the office here. We've been trying to iron out what's going on with our network and some other stuff. Oh, and I ran by Sally's residence and spoke to one of her neighbors."

"What was Sally's house like? It sounded like she left Jason's farm pretty quickly. Did it look like she had a good place lined up?"

"Definitely. She had an apartment in that new building that overlooks the lake. Upscale with views. Clearly, she was doing financially well off the book," said Grayson.

"Was her neighbor able to give any information?"

Grayson said, "Not really. She was dying to help, though. I could tell she was trying to scrape up any helpful tidbits she could think of. But since Sally was such a new neighbor, she was only able to give her impression of her."

"Which was?"

"The neighbor wasn't a fan," said Grayson with a chuckle. "Sally wasn't friendly but kept to herself. She thought Sally must have something to hide because she acted so furtive. The neighbor thought maybe she was snooty because she had a bestselling book."

I sighed. "That's what people always say about introverted people. And I think it's rarely the case."

"Right. I'm sure it was more the fact that Sally just wasn't interested in mixing and mingling with the neighbors. At least she could give me a couple of quotes for the paper tomorrow. Speaking of which, I've got to run. How about if we shoot for coffee tomorrow morning? You're working, right?"

"That's what Wilson texted me while I was at the store. The police are letting the library operate as usual tomorrow. I'm opening up, so I'll need to be at the library by eight to get everything set up for the day."

"How about seven, then?" asked Grayson. "Will that give you enough time?"

"Perfect. That way I can run back home and pick up Fitz before heading to the library. See you then."

And, to Fitz's delight, I spent the rest of the afternoon with him and *Don Quixote* on the sofa.

The next morning, I headed out to meet Grayson at Keep Grounded, our local coffee shop. Walking in the door always brightened my day a little. It was always cheerful and bright in there with light streaming through the many windows and upbeat jazz music playing. The coffee shop had gone up for sale after the death of the owner, Rufus, and was bought out by one of his employees, Tara Fuller. Tara and I were friends, and it made me happy to see her doing so well. She had her dark hair up in her customary ponytail and sported an apron with "Keep Grounded" and a coffee cup logo on it.

Grayson wasn't there yet when I walked in, and the shop was pretty quiet. Tara greeted me with a smile. "How are things going, Ann?" Then she frowned. "Oh, maybe they're not actually going well. I heard about what happened at the library yesterday."

I nodded. "Yes, yesterday was pretty rough."

"Wasn't Sally there to speak, too? She had an event there?"

I said, "That's right. But it didn't happen *during* the program. It was afterwards." Which wasn't honestly much better. "Did you know her at all?"

"Just a little. Sally kept to herself. I know she liked a basic cup of medium roast with room for cream. Aside from that, though, she was pretty much a mystery to me."

"Was she a regular?" I asked.

"Every Sunday, like clockwork."

That made sense. The library was closed on Sundays. If Sally had kept to a strict writing schedule, she would have wanted a place to go on Sundays, too.

"She'd get a single cup of coffee and nurse it for hours while she worked." Tara bobbed her head to indicate a small table against the wall. "If someone else was in the spot, she looked like she'd been thrown for a loop. It was almost as if she had to figure out what to do next."

I said, "She was definitely a creature of habit. She was usually sitting in the same spot at the library, too."

The bell on the door rang, and I turned to see Grayson coming in. He grinned at us both. "How're things going?"

"I was just talking to Ann about Sally."

Grayson raised his eyebrows. "Sally was a regular here, too? I know she was at the library most of the time."

"She was only at the coffee shop when the library was closed," said Tara.

"By herself?" asked Grayson, ever the reporter.

Tara said, "Most of the time. Sometimes her boyfriend would join her—Jason, from the farm stand. Sally always looked pretty displeased when he was there."

I asked, "Because he was interrupting her work? Or did you get the impression she wasn't really as into him as he was into her?"

"Both. The funny thing was that Jason seemed totally oblivious to it. He was just happy to spend time with her, even if she was working, and he was simply sitting next to her." Then Tara gave them a smile. "By the way, I've got someone right now that I'm seeing who makes *me* happy to spend time with him."

I opened my eyes wide. "Really? That's great! Who is he?"

Tara chuckled, "I had to import him, since there aren't too many options available in Whitby. His name is Harrison, and he's from Belton."

Belton was a neighboring town to Whitby, with a picturesque downtown and a few nice restaurants.

"That's great, Tara," Grayson said, echoing me. "How did you meet him?"

"I was at a restaurant there, waiting for a friend of mine to join me. He and I got to talking and hit it off. He invited me to go to coffee and of course I brought him here." Tara shrugged and gave us a happy smile. "Things sort of progressed from there."

"We'll have to all go out for dinner sometime," I said.

The bell on the door rang again and a large group of women came in.

"We'd better let you go," I added. We gave her our coffee orders and settled down at one of the tables.

"Busy day here," said Grayson as several more people came in.

We chatted for a couple of minutes until our coffees were ready. Grayson picked them up and brought them to the table.

We were talking about odds and ends when the door opened once again. This time the person coming in made my eyes widen a bit.

"Someone you know?" asked Grayson.

"It's Liv Nelson. Burton mentioned wanting to speak with her in connection with the case. I wonder if he's been able to find her."

Regardless, Liv looked rougher than I'd ever seen her. She must either have been ill or worried. Her skin was so pale it was almost waxy. She got her coffee and then spotted me and started walking in our direction.

I introduced Grayson and Liv and then invited Liv to sit with us.

"I'm glad you're here, Ann. I wanted to ask you about what went on in the library yesterday."

"With Sally? Awful, isn't it? Did you know her?"

"Not really. I mean, I'd see her in the library sometimes and we'd chat for a few minutes. But it wasn't as if we were friends or anything." She took a deep breath, realizing the words were spilling out of her too fast. "Sorry. I'm really rattled right now. You can probably tell."

"What's going on?" I asked, concerned.

"The police have been leaving messages on my phone. I'm not even sure how they got the number. I mean, why are they trying to get in touch with me?"

Grayson said, "They're probably just trying to reach out to everybody who spends time at the library and might have known Sally."

His answer seemed to make Liv relax for a few moments, but then she was tightly wound again. "I don't know. They seem pretty persistent. Why would they keep trying to reach out unless they thought I was somehow involved in all this?"

"You haven't picked up the phone to find out?" I asked.

Liv shook her head. "I didn't want to speak with the police without a lawyer. But I have no idea who I should get to help me out." She looked at me. "Could you give me a hand with that, Ann? You do a lot of research."

"I've actually researched local attorneys for someone before. I can dig that out again and see if it needs updating. Do you need a criminal attorney?"

A few tears slid down Liv's cheeks. "I'm not sure."

Grayson said, "Do you have an alibi for yesterday morning? That would definitely stop the police from thinking you're somehow involved."

Liv looked miserable. "No, I don't. I mean, I was at work yesterday, of course. But the doctor's office I'm a receptionist for is close. From what I've heard, I'd have been on my lunch break then, anyway. So that's not going to be any help."

I knew Liv was a big reader, so I asked what was really on my mind—about the book. Sally's book seemed as if it could be key to her death. "Did you read Sally's book?"

Liv's pale face turned even paler. "Her book? I did, yes. Mostly just out of interest since I'd seen her in the library working on it for months." She cleared her throat. "Actually, when I was reading it, I noticed there were a lot of similarities to something that *I'd* written."

Grayson's eyes met mine for a second.

"I didn't realize you were a writer, Liv," I said slowly.

"Oh, I do a lot of writing at school." Her words came out stumbling, haltingly, as opposed to how they were spilling out of her earlier.

"For a Master of Education?" I frowned. "Or have I gotten that wrong?"

Liv seemed flustered. "We just do a lot of different kinds of writing for it."

"Got it. You'll have to come along to the writing group that meets once a week at the library. It's a great group of people."

Patches of scarlet now appeared on Liv's expressive face. "I don't think I could do that, Ann. I'm not all that great of a writer, and I'd feel really uncomfortable being in a group of people who practice writing all the time."

"They're not like that at all. I'm not a writer, but I hop in there with them sometimes to update my journal. They're very welcoming and supportive. Plus, they're at all different points of their writing journey. Some of them are newbies but some of them have gotten to the stage where they have very polished work. So you shouldn't feel uneasy at all about joining them."

"I'll keep that in mind." Liv gave a tight smile.

Grayson said, "Did you share your writing with Sally?"

Liv gave him a startled look as if she'd almost forgotten he was there. "What?"

"I was just wondering if you'd shared your writing with Sally. You'd mentioned that Sally had stolen some of your ideas."

Liv's voice was harsh. "I didn't mean it like that. I just meant that they were very similar. And I never showed anything to her, although I just told her what I was working on when we were both at the library one day."

She drew her breath in as a hiss, and Grayson and I turned to see Burton come in. His gaze scanned the room before settling on Liv.

"Oh no," muttered Liv.

I said, "Remember, they're just trying to gather information, Liv. They want to figure out who's behind Sally's death and finding out who she was and why she might have died is a big help in doing that."

Liv nodded and took a deep breath as Burton joined us.

"Grayson, Ann," he said politely in greeting. Then he looked at Liv. "Miss Nelson, we've been trying to get in touch with you. That's why I came in here when I saw your car parked outside."

He must really have been wanting to speak with Liv if he took the time to find out what type of car she drove.

Liv must have thought the same because she blanched. "I'm sorry. I just thought I might need a lawyer. I panicked."

Burton pulled up a chair to sit with us. He tilted his head to one side. "Now why would you need a lawyer? I'm just wanting to see if I can find out a little information from you. We're trying to get to the bottom of Sally's death as soon as possible. As someone who knew her, you should understand that."

"But I didn't know her," said Liv, her voice high. "I was just *acquainted* with her."

Burton nodded and said in a soothing voice, "I understand. It's just that I've heard you have a manuscript that's very similar to Sally's?"

"Who told you that?" asked Liv, looking startled.

Burton continued calmly, "We'd like to take a look at it."

"I don't have it anymore. I destroyed it."

Burton quirked an eyebrow. "Really? After spending so much time on it? Did you get a bad grade on it or something?"

Liv shrugged. "No. I was just embarrassed over the quality of it. Like I was just telling Ann, I'm not much of a writer. It wasn't something I wanted to keep and look back on later. So I just deleted it."

Burton nodded. "Okay. Maybe you can help me out with some other aspects of our investigation. We're trying to figure out who might have wanted to do Sally harm. We're asking everyone if she'd mentioned having trouble with someone."

"I didn't even know her," said Liv quickly.

I shifted uncomfortably in my chair. That wasn't exactly what Liv had told us.

Burton, an expert at reading people, noticed my discomfort. He said, "After all the time you spend in the library? I'd have thought you'd have at least spoken to Sally once or twice."

Liv appeared to be doing some quick thinking. Maybe she reached the conclusion that it would be better for her to divert attention to someone else and admit to an acquaintance with Sally in the process.

"There's Donna Price," she said finally. "You could always ask her about Sally."

Chapter Eight

Burton pulled out his little notepad and scribbled the name down. "Why might Donna have had a problem with Sally?"

Liv held up her hands. "I don't know. All I know is that Sally had an argument with her one day. It was pretty loud for the quiet area and other people were shushing them. Clearly, Donna had some sort of history with Sally. And, really, that's all I know." Liv stood up, clutching her coffee cup as if it were a lifeline. "I'm going to leave now."

It was more of a question than a statement.

Burton nodded. "Okay. Thanks for the help, Miss Nelson."

Liv bolted out of the coffeeshop.

Burton said wryly, "I get the impression Liv Nelson isn't fond of talking with police officers. Were the two of you able to get anything of interest before I came in?"

Grayson and I looked at each other. I said, "She was kind of a wreck, wasn't she?"

Grayson nodded. "Liv was very concerned about the police considering her a suspect."

Burton said, "Yeah, I figured that when she said she wanted a lawyer."

"Do you think she has something to hide?" I asked.

"It sure looks that way, doesn't it?"

I said slowly, "This thing about the manuscript is weird. First off, why would she be writing a long essay in a Master of Education class? I'd think she'd be focusing on shorter papers involving matters relating to education. Not something about a past crime. It just doesn't seem to tie in."

Burton sighed. "Nothing seems to tie in. I totally agree with you—that's a weird topic for the classes she's taking. But she didn't say it was something she was working on in her free time."

Grayson said, "No. And she made a big deal about not being a very good writer, so it sounds like that's not something she'd even choose to do in her spare time."

Burton stood up. "Good seeing you two. I've got to head on out."

Grayson smiled at him. "Any official updates on the investigation for the paper?"

Burton snorted. "Not yet, although you get points for asking. I'll be sure to let you know first when we have something to report."

"Good try," I said to Grayson with a grin as Burton left the coffeeshop.

"While I'm on the subject of statements, do you think Wilson would be open to a quote for the paper? Something official about Sally's death?"

I made a face. "Probably not. He's trying to distance the library from it as much as possible. Which is going to be impossible to do, of course, because there's going to be a lot of press attention on it."

Grayson nodded. "I've already seen TV news trucks from big cities here. It's not a surprise—it's a big story, after all. A bestselling writer isn't murdered in a library very often."

I said, "I'll bring it up with him, anyway. I know he'd much rather speak with you than with outside press. After all, it's the local library he's trying to protect, so it only makes sense he'd want to speak with the Whitby newspaper. It might be smart for us to try to get ahead of things with a statement instead of looking as if we're on the defensive."

"Did you bring up Mona's idea about the seed library yet?"

I shook my head. "I didn't speak with him again yesterday, except to hear the police had given the all-clear for us to open today. Maybe Mona's already mentioned it to him, but I'll ask just in case. That should be a good program for us to get good community involvement. Plus, it sounds kind of fun. I just need to research how it would work. I guess we'd need to have some sort of small greenhouse."

"A greenhouse? Won't that be a huge project?"

I shook my head. "It wouldn't be like a traditional greenhouse. We'd have some kind of artificial light source and maybe some PVC-type of irrigation. I've seen stuff like it before online, like Mona was mentioning. But I need to look more into it." I looked at my watch and made a face. "And now I guess I'd better head out. I'll see you later, won't I? At Roger Young's event?"

Now it was Grayson making a face. "Yeah, I'll be there. I have to be, since the guy is running for state senate. Although that's not my favorite type of event to cover. Politicians are always so oily. They say one thing and just do whatever they please as soon as they're elected. But I'll be covering it and take a few pictures. My photographer has another event to shoot."

"You mentioned not liking political stories. What *is* your favorite type of event?" I asked curiously.

He grinned at me. "Something that isn't work-related. Which reminds me: I was wondering if you'd be interested in going on a cheap date with me."

I chuckled. "Cheap dates are what I'm all about! I'm used to schlepping around town on the cheap—I'm a librarian. What did you have in mind?"

"I was thinking about us getting some exercise and experiencing a blast from the past at the same time."

I said, "Doing?"

"Roller skating." He grinned again but looked a little uncertain at the same time. "I was thinking about it yesterday when I drove past the building. What do you think? I haven't been skating since I was a kid."

"I think it sounds like fun. And also like we might be hugging the wall for a while; I haven't been on skates since I was a kid, either."

"Maybe in a couple of weeks?" he asked. "After things have quieted down a little at the newspaper?"

"It's a date."

We headed out to our cars and went our separate ways. I headed back home to collect Fitz, load him in his carrier, and drive to the library. When I pulled up to the library, there was a woman there waiting outside the building. I sighed. That was never a good sign.

I unloaded Fitz and my laptop bag and walked toward the building.

The woman quickly approached me. "Do you work here?"

"I do . . . I'm Ann. We're not quite open yet, though."

The woman ignored this. "I need some help. I accidentally dropped off my child's school library book here yesterday. I need to get it back."

I gave her a tight smile. "Like I said, we're not quite open yet. Maybe you could wait in your car until we are?"

"What time do you open?"

"Nine o'clock." It was on all the doors and hardly a secret.

The woman heaved a gusty sigh as if I'd just intentionally ruined her day. "That's twenty minutes away."

I nodded. "I'll be happy to help you then."

If I made an exception for one person, I'd have plenty of others in the next twenty minutes. There were always a handful of people waiting for us to open. Besides, there were plenty of things I needed to do to get the library ready before I unlocked the doors. Turning on lights, copiers, logging into computers, and emptying the book depository outside. I figured I'd do the book drop box last or else the woman might harass me the entire time I was doing it.

I unlocked the door and set Fitz's carrier down. He walked out and trotted toward his favorite sunbeam. I ran through the opening procedures and then let the woman in. As I figured, there were four or five others who were right behind her.

I smiled at her. "You were saying you'd accidentally dropped off your child's school library book?"

"That's right. Did you come across it yesterday?"

I shook my head. "We closed early yesterday. You dropped it off in the morning, I'm guessing?" She must have, unless she used the book drop.

The woman nodded. "I was here right when you opened. It seems like somebody would have noticed that it wasn't part of your collection."

"Do you know the title of the book?"

She shook her head, curls bouncing.

"What the book looked like? Or what the subject was?"

She said impatiently, "I don't have any idea. It would be whatever book doesn't belong here."

I bit back another sigh. The problem with that was going to be I'd have to go through stacks of books that needed to be shelved and look through them for any that didn't seem to have our label on it. I explained that and then disappeared into a room to look through the returns. No one had had the chance to do much shelving yesterday and there were lots of books that weren't even on the carts yet. If only Zelda had volunteered yesterday afternoon, it wouldn't have been a problem. She was lightning fast.

Finally, I found the errant book, a picture book about the moon. The woman snatched it back from me with a grudging thanks and took off quickly. It wasn't a very promising start to the day.

Things picked up after that, though. A bunch of volunteers came in to attack the shelving. I could get on the computer and look up what other libraries had done with the seed lending. It looked like one library had a swap program where patrons brought in seedlings and took home others. They had all sorts of different kinds of selections, from heirloom seeds to open-pollinated plants.

I was surprised when Burton popped by for a few minutes to pick up a nonfiction book he had on hold.

"How's it all going?" I asked him as he came up to the desk to check the book out.

"With the case?" Burton made a face. "Early stages right now. I never sleep great when I've got an investigation going, so I figured maybe this book would help me out. I get pretty strung out when there's an active case."

"How are things going for you?" I asked. "I haven't had the chance to talk with you for a while lately."

Burton said, "Oh, pretty good. Aside from this case, of course. It's pretty stressful trying to track down a murderer."

"I'm sure it's got to be."

He continued, "I just wish there had been actual witnesses. Seems hard to believe that nobody noticed anything in the library. And there's not a lot of physical evidence, although we've got a couple of things we're working on."

"Anything useful?"

He nodded. "I'm sure it'll be useful for charging somebody, but the evidence we've collected doesn't match anybody we've got in our database. So it sounds like whoever murdered Sally Simmons might have been a first-time offender. Or somebody who just was never caught if he committed any other crimes."

I said, "That's all on the business side. But how have things been going for you personally?"

I'd been wanting to ask him for a while, but I'd been reticent, not wanting to put him in a sad mood. After Luna broke up with Burton, he'd been down in the dumps for a long stretch. He'd been crazy about Luna, and they'd seemed like a good match for a while. But ultimately, he wasn't exactly right for Luna. She needed someone a little more spontaneous and a little quirky. Someone more like Jeremy.

I was relieved to see that Burton lit up when I asked how his personal life was going. He said a little shyly, "Well, it's probably too early to say. But things are looking up. I met somebody at my exercise class."

My smile widened. "That's amazing! I didn't even know you were in an exercise class."

"Oh, just over at the YMCA. There's a Pilates class and my doctor told me it would help me out if I could do Pilates once a week." He snorted. "I'm the only guy in there."

"Maybe you need to spread the word," I said wryly. I paused. "So you ended up inviting this woman out?"

Burton sighed. "Well, it's taken some time. We started chatting after class one day in the parking lot. She's a teacher and got divorced a couple of years ago. We've just been friendly, you know. But I'm thinking it might be time for me to actually ask her on a date."

"Like to dinner?"

He shook his head, eyes wide as if I'd suggested he take the woman on a date to a sewer treatment plant. "No, no. That's too much too early. I was thinking it would be good to start slow, you know? Like coffee."

That certainly did seem slow. I wondered if maybe he still felt burned from the failed relationship with Luna. But I nodded and said, "That sounds nice. So you'd ask her if she wanted to go right from class over to the coffeeshop? To make it sound spontaneous?"

Burton looked relieved that I'd immediately grasped the concept. "That's it, exactly. Spontaneous. Then we can see how that goes. If everything goes well and it's not awkward at all, I could suggest that we meet up for lunch at some point."

Glaciers moved faster than Burton. But I said, "That sounds like a good plan. What's her name?"

"Belle." He said the name with reverence.

"What's she like? I mean, from what you can tell. I know you haven't spent much time with her yet." I was curious to hear if Burton had reverted to type and had a crush on someone who was similar to Luna. Was she quirky and outgoing?

Burton said, "She's kind of reserved, I guess you'd say? Quiet. But she has this amazing smile."

Reserved and quiet sounded like the polar opposite of Luna. But maybe that would work out best. With Luna and Burton, opposites had initially attracted, but the differences in their personalities had meant that the relationship didn't last for long.

Burton looked more cheerful on his way out of the library than he had on the way in. I crossed my fingers that Belle would be the right woman for him.

Chapter Nine

I was back to working on the newsletter when Wilson came over to the desk. "You're helping with the program today, aren't you?"

I nodded. "I'll be setting out muffins and starting the coffee in about thirty minutes."

Wilson looked exhausted. I had the feeling he'd probably been up most of the night, worrying about the library. I said, "Hey, Mona had a great idea for programming. A seed library. I think it'll work great as a long-term program here." I explained how the indoor greenhouse would be a converted cabinet with lights and a humidifier, gave an estimate on potential costs, and offered ideas on implementation and engagement.

Finally, I said, "What do you think?"

Wilson looked much peppier now. "It's a great idea, Ann."

I said, "It was all Mona, actually. She'd read something about it. I just did some research to see how it would work."

"Cost-effective, sustainable, and community-building. Yes, I think it'll work really well. And the board of trustees will be pleased, too."

Wilson was always eager to make the trustees happy. I could tell he was going to let them know about the new program as soon as he could.

He continued, "I was just about to ask you to plan as much programming as possible. I think we need to get patrons back into the library posthaste."

I nodded. "I'll be sure to work on library promo ideas today when I get a chance."

He looked relieved. "Good. And, of course, we should make sure today's program goes smoothly. We always want to make the local politicians happy."

Then, just as soon as he'd appeared, he disappeared again into his office.

I was getting started on the promo work before when an attractive, petite woman walked jauntily into the library and came right up to the reference desk.

"Hi there!" she said in a perky voice to me.

I smiled at her. "Can I help you?"

"I hope so. I wanted to propose a special event for the library," said the woman. She laughed. "Let me introduce myself first. I'm Donna Price."

I returned the introduction. Wilson had just been talking about the need for extra programming, so I wanted to hear her out. Unfortunately, sometimes the patrons' ideas weren't really sound ones or weren't things the library wanted to take on. "What was your idea for programming?"

She beamed at me. "A fair."

I relaxed a little. Craft fairs were fairly commonplace. They were juried and didn't involve selling goods. "You'd be showcasing things like quilts, knitting, handmade jewelry . . . that type of thing?"

Donna looked horrified at the thought. "Oh no, nothing like that. No, these would be very polished items. Professional looking. And the atmosphere would have more of a party feel to it."

I had an uneasy feeling she was talking about home party businesses. "So what types of things are you proposing to display?"

"Makeup and beauty products, dietary supplements, clothing, and kitchen goods." Donna smiled at me. "It would be a home business fair."

I shook my head. "I'm afraid the library has a policy about that type of thing."

Donna pressed her lips together tightly in displeasure. Then she said, "I'd like to speak with your manager, please."

Fortunately, Wilson was just leaving his office, likely to see why I wasn't going ahead and setting up the community room for Roger Young's event. I motioned him over and Wilson introduced himself pleasantly.

Donna reiterated her idea for a "home business fair" and I saw Wilson's expression grow cautious. Donna must have noticed it too because she said, "I know the library must want to support small businesses."

Wilson said, "Unfortunately, what you're talking about *aren't* small businesses. They're large businesses. The businesses are the ones making most of the profit."

Donna was clearly displeased by this. "They're women with families. They're just looking for more flexible work."

"And it's good that they have some options for extra income. But most libraries operate within certain parameters. We have express policies against anything for-profit unless it's a single professional. A tax preparer, a single author selling books, that sort of thing." His voice softened a bit, perhaps because Donna was now looking quite sour. "Unfortunately, that's what we're working with. I'm sorry we can't be of more help. If you'll excuse me?"

And Wilson hurried off to the children's section, which is where he'd been heading before I'd flagged him down.

Donna said to me, "You'll have to change his mind. This is the kind of event that would be very popular here in Whitby."

"There's no changing Wilson's mind, I'm afraid. He's in charge."

Donna gave a sharp hiss through her teeth. "It seems to me the library could use something positive right now. An event that could bring the community together. The *last* event you held here didn't exactly have a good outcome. The library could use some good PR right now after the whole 'death in the library' thing."

I was eager to get away from the home business fair topic. "Yes. We're working on PR now. Did you know Sally Simmons?"

"Oh, just barely, you know. Of course, that didn't stop our over-zealous police department from talking with just about everybody in town, that I can see. Even pestering ideal citizens like myself."

This was interesting. Burton and the state police certainly didn't have time to "pester everyone," despite what Donna had said. If they'd spoken with her, there was a reason.

Donna must have misinterpreted my interest as something else, because she quickly said, "No worries, I was busy working when Sally died. At home, since I have a stay-at-home job."

I wasn't sure Burton would have thought that was much of an alibi, but I nodded.

"Anyway, like I said, I only knew Sally a little. It wasn't as if we had lunch sometimes or a coffee. She and I had absolutely nothing in common."

I had to agree with that. From what I'd seen of Sally and her introversion and Donna with her pushy bravado, the two didn't seem to have much in common at all. "Did you two go to school together?" I asked politely.

Donna's eyes narrowed. "What makes you think that?"

She definitely seemed wary about how she and Sally had known each other. "Only that you seemed to be about the same age."

Donna relaxed. "Yes, we knew each other from school. But only in passing, you know. Asking what we'd missed from class if we'd been absent one day—that sort of thing."

I suddenly remembered I'd seen Donna at Sally's program. "It was nice of you to attend the library event and support Sally. Especially since you didn't know her well."

Donna flushed. "Well, I'd read the book, of course. *Everyone* has read the book, haven't they? I was curious to hear more about it, and since I have a flexible schedule, I decided to hear more. It's very interesting how a writer comes up with all their ideas, isn't it? I wanted to hear how Sally got her ideas." She snapped her mouth shut as if she thought she was speaking too much.

"Are you interested in writing, too?" I asked.

Donna gave a short laugh and shook her head. "No. I mean, I'm a creative person, but not in that way. I just was interested in hearing how she did it. That's all."

"Sally gave a great talk. I wish she could have gone on writing. Who knows what she'd have been able to accomplish if she'd had time?"

Donna said, "Have you gotten any impression on how the police are doing with the investigation? I'm sure the library must want it to be wrapped up as soon as possible."

I shook my head. "I'm not sure. I know they're working hard to find out who's behind this."

"The motive must have been money, don't you think? According to what I saw in the newspaper, Sally made a six-figure advance on the book. Isn't money supposed to be the reason most people commit murder?"

"I suppose it is," I said mildly.

"I remember Sally had a brother. From when I was at school," said Donna. "I wonder if the police have spoken with him. I don't remember the two of them having much money growing up. Maybe he was ready to have more opportunities."

Donna spoke of this casually, as if it were common for a brother to murder his sister.

I just nodded. At this point, it was time for me to set up the community room for the senate candidate. My mind was already thinking of all the things I needed to do.

Donna might have realized that, because she swiftly said, "Let me know if Wilson reconsiders the fair. I'll check in with you later."

To my surprise, instead of leaving, Donna headed over to the periodicals section and found something to read. She wasn't a regular here, but it was always good to see a patron relaxing here for a while.

I started with the setup, pulling chairs and tables out, putting the lectern in place, checking the microphone, and setting out the food and beverages.

Wilson stuck his head in and nodded, looking satisfied with my progress. "Looks like everything is in place. Is Grayson planning on being here?"

I nodded. "It sounded like he was going to run a story on the event."

Fitz walked into the room to see where I was and if it involved cat food.

Wilson beamed at him. "There's the star of the library. I hear more compliments about Fitz than I do about our programs."

"That's because Fitz loves people. He's a very unusual cat."

"Like you've said before, Ann, he's almost like a therapy animal. I've seen him cuddling up with some of our most crotchety patrons and making them smile." Wilson paused and said, "Which reminds me. Are you doing okay? It occurred to me that you might have known Sally, apart from the library. You were of a similar age, weren't you?"

I nodded. "Similar, but not exact. We didn't know each other."

Wilson looked relieved. "Got it. I was sort of horrified at the idea last night that you might have and that I should have offered you some time off." He paused. "*Do* you need some time off?"

I shook my head. "No need for that. Besides, the library has always been my happy place."

Wilson again looked relieved. I had no doubt he was genuine in his offer for me to take some time off, but he was very glad he wasn't going to have to figure out staffing around an absence. Fitz wrapped himself around his leg, and Wilson reached down to give him a rub. "Is Fitz going to stick around and listen to the candidate?"

"It's unlikely. He's not fond of a full community room. He'd rather approach people one-on-one," I said.

At that point, Roger Young came into the room. He was a classically good-looking guy with blond hair, blue eyes, and a perennial tan. He'd dressed the part as the local politician and was wearing a suit with a red and blue tie.

Wilson immediately left my side to speak with him, as I expected he would. I got a few more things in place in the room and then opened the door for the public. Looking at the number of people milling around outside the room, it looked like it was going to be another big event. You could never predict how these things might go. Sometimes we did all the right things on our end and the community just wouldn't show up. This didn't seem to be the case today.

I looked out into the library and saw Linus over in the periodical section. He was in his favorite armchair and was reading a book. He was very much a fan of a schedule and would start out with the newspapers before delving into the book of the moment. I noticed Donna was no longer sitting near him. A couple of seconds later, I saw why, as she walked into the community room.

This was another surprise. Maybe I hadn't given Donna a fair shake, but she just didn't seem like the political type. Maybe she was simply killing time—or wanted a snack. There were plenty of people over at the food table, getting a muffin or a doughnut. I could see Wilson was looking pleased at the turnout.

Grayson slipped in the door a moment later, his photographer in tow. Roger clearly recognized him—I saw him adjust his tie.

"Could I get a picture of the two of you?" Grayson asked Roger and Wilson.

Wilson looked even more pleased. He was always happy to be featured in the local paper. They posed, Roger flashing impossibly white teeth against his tan and Wilson giving a more subdued smile.

Ten minutes later, it was time for the program to start. Wilson introduced Roger, carefully reading his bio before giving him the floor. Everyone applauded and Roger smiled at them before launching into his prepared speech.

I wasn't planning on voting for Roger, but I thought he was a good speaker with excellent command of the room. He had clearly given this talk before and had a great sense of timing. He paused in all the right places for people to laugh or to make more of an impact with his words. Everyone applauded again when he wrapped up.

Then there was a question-and-answer portion. Roger was just as smooth during this part, delivering polished answers to questions he'd clearly heard before. At any rate, he'd charmed the audience, and they were eager to speak with him after the event wrapped up.

I glanced around the room as I waited for the patrons to file out so that I could put the room to rights again. Donna was still sitting in the back of the room, which was where I now remembered seeing her during Sally's program, too. She was watching Roger speak with audience members and had an expression on her face that I couldn't quite place. I wondered if she knew Roger, who was also about her age. She saw me looking in her direction and gave me a tight smile before grabbing her purse and heading out the door.

Roger was still hanging around speaking with an older woman, so I realized it would be a few minutes before I could start putting chairs away and cleaning up the food and drinks. I didn't want Roger to feel like I was rushing him out, and the older woman seemed to be chatty. Instead, I stepped out of the room and headed back to the reference desk.

Ten minutes later a teen came up to me, looking apologetic. "Sorry, I used these books for a paper I'm writing, and I can't figure out where to return them on the shelves."

I smiled at her. "That's no trouble at all. You're smart to just hand them to me. That way, I can put them back in the right place so others can find them."

She smiled back, took a picture of one of our flyers on teen programs, and headed out the door. I took the books back to the nonfiction section to shelve them. The teen girl had been the only student working in the area and now that she had left, it was completely quiet back there.

Quiet until I heard a thump and a furious hiss a couple of aisles down. "You're not returning my phone calls!"

Chapter Ten

Looking through the shelves, I could barely make out two people—Donna and Roger.

Roger's voice was icy in return, decidedly not the voice he was using at the event. "That's because you persist in calling me at my campaign headquarters. What do you expect?"

"I expect you to pick up! That's the only way I can get in touch with you. It's not like I have your personal number."

Roger gave an impatient sigh and recited it to her. Donna typed it into her phone.

"Calling me at work has got to stop," he said curtly. "And I need you to keep your voice down."

Donna snorted. "That's easy enough. We're at a library, after all." She paused. "Look, I know you had something to do with it. You must think I'm a fool if you don't realize that."

"I had absolutely nothing to do with Sally's death. Nothing. I've been on the campaign trail and traveling to different towns the past few weeks."

Donna said fiercely, her voice raising a little, "You read her book. You know what she wrote."

"I don't read those types of books," said Roger dismissively.

Donna's voice raised a bit more. "Then why were you there if you didn't read the book? I *saw* you there. At the book event."

"Keep your voice down," he said in a flat tone.

"You were there!" Donna didn't appear to be listening to him. She seemed like the kind of woman who was accustomed to getting her way, and she certainly seemed to want something from Roger. I remembered again her determination when she was trying to get us to break with library policy. But she was now up against a man who was also likely used to getting whatever he wanted. I could tell it was going to be a battle of wills to see who came out ahead. Whatever Donna was talking about, it was clearly making Roger uncomfortable.

"Look, I saw a TV interview where Sally discussed the book. I certainly don't have time to read with all the campaigning and traveling I'm doing. But I could get the gist of what her book was about."

Donna's voice was insistent. "You killed her to keep her quiet. Sally could end your political career, couldn't she? I can't believe you'd stoop that low. Poor Sally."

"It sounds like *you* can end my political career."

Donna paused as Roger's ominous words sank in. Then she said, "The *police* are speaking with me, Roger. The *police*. I can't believe I'm in this spot."

"You put *yourself* in that spot. It has nothing to do with me. You must have said or done something to make the cops realize you were a potential suspect."

Donna was quiet on that point and Roger kept pushing, "What happened, Donna? Did you have an argument with Sally that someone overheard? Did you tell her off in public? That's exactly the kind of thing the police are going to follow-up on with a case like this. Plus, you have just as much motive as I do. For all I know, you're trying to shift suspicion.

"You can't turn things around on me! I'm the innocent party here. I've done nothing wrong. You can't think that none of this is going to come out. You should just hang up that political career. It's over."

Roger gave a short laugh. "I can't be convicted for something I didn't do."

"Then you clearly don't read the papers. Plenty of people are wrongfully convicted all the time. I think you did it, no matter what you say. If it's not you, then who is it?"

"It was probably that dopey boyfriend of Sally's. From what I understand, he supported Sally while she was working on the book, and she dumped him as soon as she'd made it. If that's not a motive for murder, I don't know what is," said Roger.

"Why would he kill her, though? If she was alive, he could pressure her to pay him back some of the money he spent on her."

Roger shrugged. "Maybe he realized he wasn't going to get a dime from her. He could have just been furious and wanted to take his revenge."

"Or *you* might have just blown up one day and decided to end the threat to your career."

Roger said coldly, "You, of all people, should know I'm not the type to blow up. I'm always able to remain cool and collected, even in a crisis."

At that point, a group of students came in, talking loudly and heading over to the nonfiction stacks to work on a group project. Roger hastily left, and a minute later, Donna did, too. I headed back to the reference desk, feeling like my head was spinning.

Since no one was currently around the desk, I quickly called Burton to fill him in, stepping into a deserted storage room as I did.

"So Donna thought Roger was responsible for the murder," said Burton.

"That's how it sounded to me. But Roger was firing back, saying that Donna might have done it and was just trying to shift responsibility onto him."

Burton sighed. "This case is making my head hurt. But you've been a huge help, Ann. Listen, be careful. Somebody out here is probably desperate—you don't want to be the next victim."

"I'll be careful. I wasn't intentionally snooping this time, I promise . . . just shelving books. I guess Donna knew Roger was going to be at the library for his event and was trying to catch him before he left. She'd said something about not being able to reach him by phone—that he was ignoring her calls."

"Imagine that," said Burton dryly. "Well, like I said, I appreciate you filling me in. This is an angle we're definitely going to follow-up on."

I was working on the library newsletter when Grayson's friend Jeremy came into the building, a quirky smile on his face. It was always something of a day-brightener when he came over. He was the kind of person who had a lot of energy and almost an aura of it crackling around him. He smiled a lot, cracked jokes, and was just *different*. Luna clearly adored him, and they got along really well together.

"Hey there, Ann," he said with his lips quirked up in a smile. "How are things?"

"Great," I said. I couldn't help teasing him. "Here to pick up a few books."

"Oh yeah," he said with a wink. "I was thinking about getting *The Rise and Fall of the Roman Empire* for starters. I might follow that up with *War and Peace*."

"Well, I can't speak for the Roman empire, but *War and Peace* is actually an excellent read."

Jeremy nodded as if he were making a mental note. "Thanks for the recommendation. I'll check it out when I've got nothing else to do for five months. Because it'll take me about that long to plow through it."

Luna had spotted Jeremy from the children's section and walked up to join us. She beamed at him. "What's up?"

"Oh, Ann here was trying to persuade me of the merits of *War and Peace*," said Jeremy, rolling his eyes good-naturedly. "What she doesn't understand is that I'm more on the level of Dr. Seuss."

"Hey, we have some great Dr. Seuss books in the kids' section," said Luna lightly. "I'll give you a tour of them anytime. Did you stop by just to see me?"

Jeremy grinned at her. "Actually, not really. Well, sort of yes and no. I'm still on my campaign to win your mother over by any means necessary."

Despite the fact Luna's mom had had a hard time warming to Jeremy, he was always looking for ways to connect with her. The game of hearts had gone well last time. But Jeremy was definitely one of those people who really needed people to like him.

Now it was Luna's turn to roll her eyes. "Not necessary, Jeremy. Like I said, Mom thinks you're great. She just needs a little time. She had a lot of fun playing cards with all of us."

"Which is exactly why I want to take that and run with it. Build on it. I was thinking maybe I could hang out with her and do some more things she's interested in."

"Knitting?" I asked innocently.

Luna burst out laughing, and Jeremy made a face.

"Okay, well, maybe not knitting," said Jeremy. "I was thinking more along the lines of taking a nice walk?" He looked at Luna hopefully.

"She used to love taking walks, but her mobility isn't great, remember?"

Jeremy looked almost comically crestfallen. "Anything else you can think of?"

Luna quirked an eyebrow at him. "Reading is big on her list."

"That's not exactly a communal activity," said Jeremy quickly. "I wanted something that I could use to connect with Mona."

"According to our book clubs, it *is* actually a communal activity," I said with a smile. "Sorry, I know I'm not helping."

Jeremy sighed. "Let's try again. Is there anything else? Bowling?"

Luna snickered.

"Cooking?"

Luna tilted her head to one side. "Yes, but you're not much of a cook, Jeremy."

"Perfect. She could show me how."

I said, "Why don't you introduce her to one of *your* hobbies, Jeremy. Maybe that would work better."

"Weightlifting?" asked Jeremy glumly.

Luna snorted. "Weightlifting? That's one of your hobbies?"

He grinned at her. "It's a hobby I don't practice very often. And you'll notice I didn't say 'bodybuilding.' I just lift hand weights. But hey, those do the job."

I tried again. "What do you like to do when you're home after work and you're by yourself?"

Jeremy's answer was quick. "Play video games."

I chuckled. "Okay, well, that probably won't work as well."

But Luna was looking thoughtful. "I'm not so sure about that. My mom does love games."

"Yes, but they're *card* games," said Jeremy. "That's not the same thing."

Luna continued, "She also likes playing solitaire on the computer."

Jeremy and I looked at each other.

"Not really the same thing," said Jeremy again.

"Still, I think we could give it a try. You know I enjoy gaming, myself," said Luna. "I'm thinking about what kind of video game she might like playing."

Now Jeremy was looking more interested. "I see. So your mom might not like to play fighting-type games, but she might enjoy playing RPG."

I must have been looking confused because Jeremy said, "Role-playing games. Games where she can choose a character and play a part in the story world."

Luna said, "Oh, I can totally see her playing some of that stuff. She'd get so engrossed in the world that I might have trouble getting her out of it."

"We'd have to be careful of that or Wilson might get mad at us," I said wryly. "Are any of those two-person games? The whole point was that Jeremy could spend more time with your mom."

Jeremy considered this. "There's Minecraft. That would be a good multiplayer game for her."

"Do you have that? Or have you ever played it?" asked Luna.

"I used to play it a lot when I was a kid. It's been around for a while. It's a sandbox game, so you just build your world. She can raise animals on a farm or build a castle. I've got an old game and we can see if your mom is interested. She might think I'm crazy when I bring it up."

Luna shook her head. "Nope! Mom is used to craziness, although it's usually me who's the one who's being crazy. Okay, so Operation Video Game is now in progress." She glanced across the library. "And look who's coming over to say hi to us."

And indeed, Mona was leaving her sitting area and heading our way.

Jeremy gulped. "Suddenly my throat is really dry. And it feels like my tongue is filling up my mouth."

"Don't be so melodramatic," said Luna with a laugh.

Mona stopped short when she got to us. "The three of you look guilty," she said. "Were you talking about me?"

Jeremy's expression proceeded to look even guiltier, and I was sure my face looked the same. But Luna, who was apparently used to deceiving her mom, said lightly, "Us? No way. We were just talking about the investigation and wondering if they were closer to figuring out what happened to Sally."

Mona nodded but still seemed suspicious.

Luna gave Jeremy a prompting look.

Jeremy cleared his throat. "We were also talking about video games."

Mona said, "Oh gracious. Is my daughter getting you hooked on video games? I'm sorry to hear that. They're such a terrible time suck."

Jeremy looked desperately to Luna for help.

Luna said, "What? No, they're great, Mom. You know how they help me relax at the end of a long day."

Mona tilted her head to one side. "You don't even need help relaxing. You're relaxed all the time."

I had to say that was true. Even if was a wild day in the library, Luna was always relaxed and in good spirits. She was one of those people I'd seek out on a rough day because her good humor was infectious.

"True," said Luna, "but they can *transport* you. Just like books can. Jeremy likes playing games, too."

Jeremy again managed to look very guilty. And also apologetic. "I do. Sometimes."

Luna rolled her eyes at him and gave him that prompting look again.

He said, "I was wondering if you might like to play a game with me, Mona."

Mona narrowed her eyes a little, looking confused. "Me? I'm not sure video games are my thing."

I decided to try to help out. "You might want to give it a go. Luna's right—some games have a storyline just like books do. They can transport you to another world. I bet there are some games that Jeremy or Luna has that you'd really enjoy."

Jeremy said, "And I could play one of them with you." He hurriedly added, "If you'd like to, I mean."

Mona thought about this. "Well, I suppose I could give it a go. But if it's not my thing, I'm going to let you know right away. That won't hurt your feelings, will it?"

Jeremy shook his head quickly. "Not at all. I wouldn't want you doing something you don't like doing."

"There are definitely not enough hours in the day to play a game I'm not enjoying. Well, when would you like to try it out? This game?"

Jeremy said, "Uhh. I don't know. What does your schedule look like?"

Luna gave him a fond look and shook her head. I hid a smile. Mona's schedule, unless she was heading off to a doctor visit or the hairdresser, was totally up to Mona. What's more, it involved reading and knitting.

This time, I saw a hint of a smile on Mona's lips. "Well, there's no time like the present, is there? How about tonight after you get back from work? I might even be able to cook us a meal."

"That would be great. I'll bring the game over." He quickly looked at his watch and said with relief, "I better get going and head back to work. See you later, Mona. Bye everybody."

Jeremy practically skipped out the door.

"A very unusual young man," said Mona, watching him leave. "Well, I'd better get to the community room. The fellow from the local extension office is doing a talk on houseplants."

As soon as Mona walked away, Luna said, "I'm glad she went with it. I had a feeling she might."

"Because she enjoys solitaire on the computer?"

"Because I think she secretly knows she needs to figure out a way to warm up more to Jeremy. It's too bad that she was so devoted to Burton," said Luna.

"But it's not like she doesn't see Burton anymore. He's in here pretty often, and I've seen them chatting before."

Luna shrugged. "I guess it's not quite the same for her. But yeah, I think she'll like the game. She's not a very competitive person, so it was smart of Jeremy to think of a game where there's really no winning involved."

Zelda, lurking in the stacks, came out to give us a disapproving look.

"Break's over," said Luna with a laugh. "We're in trouble with Zelda now."

Chapter Eleven

The rest of the day was blissfully normal. I got plenty of information on how to set up the seed and seedling swap online and started making notes of potential costs. It was my day to leave early, so I put Fitz in his carrier at five o'clock, waved to Luna, and headed out.

I was pulling into my driveway when I got a text message from Grayson.

Have you had enough of me today, or can I bring dinner by for both of us?

I smiled and texted him back that I'd absolutely love to have both him and dinner at the house. Grayson was a good cook, and I assumed he'd made the meal. Although I'd meal-prepped and had something ready to cook for tonight, I appreciated not having to make it. Cooking for one wasn't all that interesting, and I wasn't much into it, anyway.

Grayson came over minutes later with a foil-covered rectangular dish. He pulled off the foil and beamed at me.

"Lasagna," I said happily. "How did you know I was in the mood for that?"

"I had my fingers crossed," he said with a smile. Fitz rubbed up against his legs and Grayson leaned over to rub him.

I poured us some white wine, Grayson started a jazz playlist on his phone, and we took the food into the coziness of the living room.

I asked Grayson how his day had gone, and he said, "It was pretty quiet after Roger Young's event. I mostly just laid out the copy for tomorrow's edition of the paper. How about you?"

I took a sip of wine. "It was actually pretty quiet there, too. But there was one scene that I witnessed."

I told him about Roger and Donna in the stacks and Grayson's eyes grew wide. "So our state senate candidate might be involved in a murder?"

I shrugged. "Donna certainly seemed to think it was a possibility."

"It sounds like the motive is tied into the book. A book I still haven't read." He glanced ruefully at the book he'd brought over with him. "Instead, I'm reading *The Storyteller.*"

That was musician Dave Grohl's memoir, and it was a good one. "*Guilty* is quite a different type of read."

"Could you fill me in?" he asked. "Just the headlines."

"It's about a group of college friends who cover up a murder." I raised one eyebrow over my wineglass.

Grayson gave a low whistle. "Okay. So what are we thinking? Sally started feeling guilty over the years about her involvement and decided to spill it in a book?"

"I'm thinking it's more than that. Maybe Sally somehow just knew about it but wasn't directly involved. I totally agree that the guilty feeling was there, though. Sally might have been aware of what happened and felt guilty because she never called the police or told anyone about it. After all, she named the book *Guilty.* Maybe Roger and Donna or maybe some other students were involved in the death and subsequent coverup. Maybe Sally's conscience wouldn't allow her to stay silent any longer and she brought the whole incident to light."

Grayson considered this. "Thinking back to her talk at the library, she came right out and spoke about the book as a study on guilt. I wonder if maybe one of the reasons she wrote it was to make the other *students* feel guilty."

"That could be," I said. "I also wondered if maybe she wrote the book *specifically* for them. Like that was her main purpose for writing it. That could explain the lack of promo for the story . . . the fact that Sally wasn't interested in doing a lot of book interviews or media or a book tour."

"That makes sense. So, where did this alleged crime happen? Did they all go to Whitby College?" asked Grayson. "Did you hear of any mysterious deaths taking place there?"

I could tell the wheels were already turning in his mind. After all, any story featuring a political candidate was going to be a big one. I shook my head. "I'm not sure where they went to school, but I didn't hear about any murders at the time I was in school. I'm sure my aunt would have been worried sick, even if they hadn't been local, and would have told me about them."

I'd been raised by my great-aunt, and we'd had a great relationship. But she could be a little overprotective.

Grayson took a thoughtful bite of his lasagna and considered this. "How about if we go see Donna tomorrow? Are you off?"

"I'm on the schedule to work tomorrow, but I don't go in until just around lunchtime."

"Perfect. Now we just need an excuse to go talk with her." He grinned at me. "Otherwise, we'll look like the crazy newspaper editor and librarian."

"Donna was trying to get Wilson to agree to a sales event at the library earlier for some of those home party businesses. Maybe we could approach her on finding out what it's like to work for one of those companies." I made a face. "It's not a great pretext, but Donna was so eager, I think she'd jump on it."

"That sounds like it could work. I could tell her I was trying to get information for a potential story so that way I'm not totally locked in," said Grayson.

"Are you going to call her to set up a time?"

He shook his head. "I'd rather catch her a little off-guard. But I obviously don't want to wake her up or anything. Do you think 9:30 would work tomorrow?"

"That sounds good to me."

With the plans made, we set about finishing up the lasagna and wine. Even later, we snuggled up on the sofa with Fitz and our books for the rest of the evening.

The next morning, I was up early to get a few things done before Grayson came over and before I needed to get to work. I tidied up around the house, emptying the dishwasher, putting laundry away, and taking out the trash. Then I hopped in the car and quickly ran a couple of errands, marveling how new errands always seemed to spring up as soon as I'd finished others.

By the time I got back, I barely had time to run a comb through my hair and change into work clothes before Grayson appeared to take us by Donna's house.

He leaned over and gave me a quick kiss as I climbed into his car.

"How was your morning?" he asked.

"Productive," I said with a smile.

"Not relaxing?"

"Relaxing was last night. This morning, it was all about getting things knocked out." I paused. "I'm hoping the trip to see Donna isn't going to mess up our morning mojo."

Grayson looked over at me curiously before looking through the windshield again. "You're feeling a little anxious about it?"

"Not *really*. I mean . . . well, okay, yes." I ended with a chuckle. "That's actually exactly what I'm feeling."

Grayson reached over to hold my hand. "Hey, you don't have to come along for this at all. You're not a member of my newspaper staff, you know. I can drop you off back home."

I gave him a wry smile. "The thing is that I want to be there and hear what she has to say."

"But be more like a fly on the wall?"

"Maybe," I admitted. "I don't have the whole gonzo reporting experience like you do."

Grayson said, "That's understandable. If it makes you feel any better, I'm just planning on starting out with telling her you mentioned she had a small business, and I was collecting information for a story. The segue to murder will happen later."

"You always do a good job. I'll be fine."

But I found as we pulled up in front of Donna's cheerful white-brick house and riotous flowerbed that my hands were clammy. Was it because she'd been so pushy when she'd asked

Wilson and me to hold a fair? Or was it because of that heated conversation she'd had with Roger in the stacks the day before?

Grayson was collecting his notebook, pen, and a recording device. "What did you make of her, by the way?"

"Donna? I was just thinking about that. I didn't like her much at all, to be honest. But then, to be fair, I guess I didn't see her at her best. She didn't want to take no for an answer when she was asking about a home business fair. And she sounded furious when she was talking with Roger later." I thought about this. "Furious, but also maybe a little afraid."

Grayson shot me a quick look as we got out of the car. "Afraid of Roger?"

I could tell he saw this story getting bigger and bigger.

"I don't know. Maybe a little? But I think it was mainly that she was afraid of the whole situation. Of being considered a suspect, talking to the police. Of having someone out there who was a murderer."

We walked up a brick pathway to the house. A wreath that might have been handmade bedecked the front door, which had been painted a cheerful blue.

Grayson gave me a wink, which settled my nerves. "Here goes nothing," he said.

He rang the doorbell, and nothing happened. He frowned. "I could hear the doorbell ringing inside."

"Her car's here," I noticed. "At least, there *is* a car here. I'm just assuming it's hers."

"Did she live alone?"

I said, "I don't think so. There was some mention of a husband and children, I thought. But maybe she was just speaking figuratively. She said that these businesses were helpful for the women who needed to help support their families."

Grayson glanced at his watch. "Just after nine-thirty. Maybe she's showering or something."

I felt my sense of uneasiness grow. "I don't know. She seemed like the type of person who got up early and started right in with her day. She was at the library pretty early yesterday."

Grayson looked more closely at me. "Are you okay?"

I shook my head. "I have a bad feeling about this. My gut is telling me something's wrong."

Grayson nodded. "In journalism school, we were always taught to go with our gut." He hesitated. "I don't feel right about trying the door to see if we can walk in, but we could look around back. She's obviously into gardening. Maybe she's tending to the beds out there."

So we walked around the side of the house. A cat watched us with interest from behind a bush.

And that's where we found Donna Price—dead. A golf club lay on the ground beside her.

Chapter Twelve

We called Burton right away and, to his credit, he was there almost immediately. The state police, already around because of the investigation into Sally's death, were at the house just a few minutes later. Grayson and I told them where to look and soon grim-looking officers were stringing up crime scene tape.

Grayson had his arm around me as we stood on the sidewalk in front of Donna's house. He said gruffly, "Your gut knew what it was talking about."

I nodded. "I wish it hadn't. I mean, Donna hadn't made a great impression on me, but I didn't want anything to happen to her." I looked up at Grayson. "I guess this means Roger is going to be the main suspect. After all, he was having quite an argument with her yesterday. I wonder if Burton got the chance to talk to both of them after I filled him in."

"Looks like you'll have the opportunity to ask him yourself."

Sure enough, Burton was heading our way with a somber look on his face.

"Rough way to start out the morning," he said to us sympathetically. "Although I do have to wonder what the two of you were doing in Donna Price's backyard."

Grayson had the grace to look flushed. "Sorry, Burton. That was my idea. After Ann told me about the scene between Donna and Roger, I thought it might be good to talk with her as a reporter. I had the excuse of her home business and pulled Ann into this."

Burton nodded. "That makes sense. You're trying to do your job, after all. If Roger Young is involved in any of this, it's going to be a huge story."

I said, "Did you have the chance to follow-up with Donna yesterday?"

Burton looked pained and shook his head. "No. The team was diverted by some physical evidence we were trying to make heads or tails of. Somebody was sent out, but there was no answer at the door." He sighed. "She might have been trying to avoid us. If she hadn't done that, maybe she'd still be alive."

Grayson said, "I suppose this means Roger Young is the prime suspect?"

"If he doesn't have an excellent alibi. Of course, the overheard conversation is hearsay now because Donna Price is dead. The guy is probably around people most of the time, though, so he might just *have* an alibi. He's got advisers and campaign staff and a whole entourage."

I said, "Was Donna married?"

Burton said, "The officer who'd tried and failed to speak with her yesterday did some background work on her. She was married but divorced. No children. She receives some alimony from her ex as well as income from her home business."

I felt a wave of sadness hit me. She'd been trying to make her own way, despite some bumps along the road.

Burton noticed my expression and quickly said, "Donna likely didn't know what hit her, literally. She was faced away from the murderer and had her earbuds in, playing music." He glanced at Grayson. "That's off-the-record, of course. As is all of this."

Grayson nodded. He wasn't that sort of reporter anyway—a fact I was very relieved about.

Burton's eyebrows went up as a car approached. "I do believe that's Roger Young now. How very interesting."

I turned around and saw Roger's face as he took in the emergency vehicles. It looked as if he was wanting to make a speedy exit, but then realized Burton had already spotted him. He parked down the street and slowly got out of his vehicle.

Burton said, "I took a quick look at Donna's phone, which was fortunately not locked. She had a bunch of missed calls and messages from Roger. I'd like to hear what that was all about."

Roger's handsome face was scowling until he got within a few yards of us. Then the politician in him couldn't seem to help but give us a gracious smile. "Burton," he said. "What's happened here?"

"Donna Price has been murdered," said the policeman, succinctly.

Roger turned a little pale under his tan. He looked covertly around him, as if ensuring the press wasn't there. He'd ignored Grayson and me when he approached, but now he looked at Grayson with narrowed eyes.

"Chief Edison, perhaps we should take our conversation somewhere more private," he said pointedly. "The house would work fine."

Burton's features flushed with irritation. "The house would certainly *not* work fine. The property is a crime scene."

Roger had the grace to look chastened. "Sorry. I'm running for public office. That's why I'm concerned about optics." His tone was lofty.

I could tell Burton was even more annoyed now. The implication was that Burton didn't follow politics.

"I realize that," said Burton in a tight voice. He was about to continue when he was called away by an officer with the state police.

Grayson murmured to me, "I'm going to step away so Roger will talk with you."

A moment later, I was alone with Roger Young.

"Are you a reporter?" There was a note of suspicion in his voice.

"A librarian."

His frown deepened as he glanced at me. "That's right. You set up the event yesterday, didn't you?"

Roger's eyes were so blue and piercing, they seemed to see right through me. He had something of a movie-star quality about him. I had the feeling that he was very much aware of how good-looking he was and never failed to use it to his advantage.

I nodded.

Roger relaxed a little. He looked absently toward Burton and rubbed his forehead. "What are you doing over here? Did you know Donna?"

"Not really. I was going to speak with her about her home business. She'd mentioned it to me in the library yesterday."

Roger cut me off quickly, decidedly disinterested in Donna's business enterprises. "This obviously has nothing to do with me. I've been at home prior to this." He seemed to be swiftly thinking. "The only reason I needed to get in touch with Donna was because she was going to help me plan another local event. I needed to find out the details so I could ensure I stayed on track and didn't fall behind schedule."

I didn't believe a word of it. I couldn't imagine another event in Whitby since he had the whole district to campaign in. Plus, I didn't see Donna as any sort of event planner.

I must have looked skeptical because I saw Roger get huffy. Before he could say anything, though, Burton slipped up behind us.

"Actually," Burton drawled, "I'd be interested in hearing more about that, too. How Donna was involved in planning a campaign event for you."

Roger shot him an irritated look. "Well, I don't know many of the details—that's why I was here, as I said. I wanted to find out more about the location, the time, and what types of snacks would be offered."

Burton nodded. "I see. It's interesting that it's the reason you're here right now. Because I've got a witness who states you had an argument with Donna Price yesterday. And it wasn't over a campaign event, either."

It might have been chicken of me, but I was relieved Burton didn't call me out. Roger's expression boded ill for the witness.

"They're lying," he spat out. "Why would I have an argument with Donna? I barely know her."

"Don't you? Because, from what the witness said, it sure sounded like you two were arguing about the book Sally Simmons wrote. That book sure has stirred up some pretty big issues from what I can tell. Something appears to have happened in the past—something her book referred to. I'd like to hear more about it."

And Burton poised his stub of a pencil over his notepad.

Roger's face was white under his tan. "They're lying," he muttered again.

"You and Donna weren't involved in something long ago? Something she was worried you were going to give away?" asked Burton, quirking an eyebrow.

"Nothing of the sort." Roger swallowed hard.

Burton considered him for a moment. "See, I have a different take on things, Roger. I'm thinking we can take this down to the station since you're so eager to have a private conversation. Of course, the way the press seems to follow you around, that might not be a place you're eager to go. I'm sure there would be lots of interesting photos."

Roger cast his gaze over at Grayson, who was hanging out by his car. Grayson nodded pleasantly at Roger.

"Okay," said Roger slowly. "But I need to have a lawyer."

"Absolutely. That's always a fine idea, especially if you might be guilty of something. Your attorney can meet us at the station."

Roger appeared to like this idea even less. He hesitated and then said reluctantly, "I suppose you might as well know. It's only going to exonerate me."

Burton patiently poised his pencil again.

Roger took a deep breath and seemed to try to organize his story for the least possible personal impact. "I knew Donna better than I do now. Now I really *do* barely know her, so I was speaking the truth. Back in college, we were friends."

"Was Sally a friend of yours, too?"

Roger shook his head impatiently. "Sally was no friend of ours. She simply turned up from time to time, but we didn't hang out with her or anything."

Burton made a careful note of this.

"So, this is what happened. Donna and I had a friend named Alan. He was the kind of friend that you'd worry about in college. Everyone partied to a certain degree, but he drank to excess." Roger pursed his lips disapprovingly. "And there were drugs involved. His friends were very concerned about his lifestyle."

Roger looked away and I couldn't help but feel he was being somewhat less than truthful. But then, he would naturally want to ensure he was shown in the best light possible.

Roger continued, "Alan came over to the house Donna was renting one night and was acting very belligerent."

"Was this normal for Alan?" asked Burton.

"When he drank, it was. He was a gentle, sort of goofy kid otherwise. He was really intelligent, but his grades were suffering because of his drug use. When Alan told me what his grades were, I knew the school probably wasn't going to invite him back the following semester. I think, deep down, Alan knew this, too. Maybe that's why his drinking and drug use got worse."

Burton nodded. "So Alan came over to see you and Donna at her place. You said he was angry?"

"Angry, but also sort of out of it. I'd never seen him that bad before. His eyes were glassy, and he was stumbling around. Donna and I were completely sober and, to be honest, it was very annoying when Alan would come by when he was wasted. I've never been a very patient person, I'm afraid."

Burton gestured with his pencil stub. "You and Donna were an item at the time, is that right? Just to clarify."

Roger shrugged. "I guess you could call us that. I think we both knew it wasn't going to last forever. Our relationship was no love match, as you can see—we're certainly not together now."

"Gotcha. Go ahead."

Roger said, "Anyway, Alan visited with us for a couple of minutes, and then staggered off to the bathroom. He knew Donna and I were anti-drugs, and I guess he wanted to dose himself up in private."

Roger had a very noble expression on as he spoke of his anti-drug stance. It was definitely Roger-the-Candidate speaking.

Burton didn't look particularly impressed. "Okay. What happened then?"

"Then Alan overdosed on heroin." Roger pressed his lips together tightly. "It was awful. Donna and I found him in the bathroom sprawled out on the floor. We couldn't believe it."

For something Roger clearly kept a secret, his words had a certain pat quality about them as if they'd been practiced numerous times.

Burton apparently picked up on this, too. I saw him frown. "Had he overdosed before?"

Roger considered this carefully. Then he slowly said, "Well, not to that extent, obviously."

"Obviously," said Burton dryly. "Since it was fatal."

Roger narrowed his eyes at him. "He'd definitely drunk before to the point of passing out, though. At first, Donna and I thought he might simply be unconscious. We tried to revive him. I even did chest compressions. But he was gone." He took a deep breath. "His parents were devastated. They didn't even realize he had a drug problem."

"This story sounds very familiar to me," said Burton, tapping the stub of a pencil on the notepad. "In fact, it sounds very much like the novel Sally wrote. I'm thinking Sally's story was more nonfiction than it was fiction."

I saw a look of surprise pass over Roger's features, and Burton press his lips together into a thin white line. It looked as if Roger was underestimating Burton again and putting him in the role of a bumbling cop who didn't really read.

Roger said, "I see. You're probably having to read her book because of the case. Look, I don't know about the details of Sally's book. I haven't read it. As I've mentioned before, I currently don't have time to read, much as I'd like to. I did hear about it online, though, and know the gist of it. I know the book was set back when I was in college. But my understanding is that her novel stated the incident was murder, not an accident at all."

Burton said tightly, "We only have your word that it *was* an accidental overdose."

Roger gave a short laugh. "Are you suggesting Alan's death was suicide? Believe me, he wasn't the type. He was a hedonist and was bent on enjoying life as much as possible. He definitely didn't want to die."

"No, I'm suggesting his death might have been murder. Or manslaughter."

This made Roger go suddenly still. "You're simply making wild guesses. You don't have any evidence of that at all."

"Well, I know it warrants further investigation. And I'd very much like to know what part Sally played in all of this. I'm guessing you and Donna didn't exactly go around campus talking about what happened."

Roger looked horrified at the idea. "Of course not. We didn't even want anyone to know we were present when it unfolded. Alan was a fun guy most of the time, and he was very popular with the student body. Most people figured he was in his dorm room when he overdosed."

Burton said, "So, if you kept it a secret, how did Sally know about it?"

Roger threw his hands up in the air. "I have no idea. I'm totally baffled. I didn't realize she knew anything at all about it. Donna said she hadn't said a word to anybody about Alan's death and neither have I."

"How did she find out?"

Roger was quiet for a few moments. "Maybe Sally somehow saw something and jumped to conclusions. I didn't know Sally, but once I saw Sally's author photo, I remembered she'd been tutoring Donna in a couple of different subjects. Maybe that night was a tutoring night, and Donna had forgotten about it."

Burton frowned. "You said Sally would just 'turn up from time to time.'"

"Yes. But the times she turned up had to do with when she was tutoring Donna."

"Is that the kind of thing Donna would do?" asked Burton. "Forget about tutoring?"

"Donna? Oh yeah, she was a total airhead when it came to keeping up with her schedule."

Burton said, "It sounds as though the two of you weren't much of a couple."

"I told you that neither of us thought it was going to last forever. We didn't have much in common."

Burton said, "So maybe it was a night Sally was supposed to be tutoring Donna. She showed up at Donna's place and you and Donna were . . . what? Talking about what had happened? Trying to revive Alan? Calling the police?"

Roger gave a frustrated shrug. "I have no idea. I never saw her there."

"Would Sally have just walked in if no one answered the door? That seems sort of unlikely for a tutor."

Roger gave another abrupt laugh. "Look, I just don't know, okay? I don't really know anything about Sally. The only people who would be able to answer your questions are Donna and Sally, and they're both dead."

"Yes," said Burton pointedly, "they are."

Now there was a note of desperation in Roger's voice, along with the arrogance. "Okay. Thinking back, when Alan joined us, the door was left ajar. He'd pushed himself into the house. And that *was* customary for Alan. He just sort of imposed himself whenever he wanted."

Burton raised his eyebrows. "But you said the two of you were friends?"

"Sure we were. He was just a sort of pushy friend. Anyway, the door was left that way until after we found Alan. We didn't want anyone walking in and running their mouth about what they'd seen, so I shut the door and called 911 right away."

Burton drawled, "It's very interesting that Sally's account of that night was so different from yours."

"That's why they call it fiction," said Roger coldly. "She made it up. Look, Chief Edison, I know people are always looking for ways to bring politicians down, but I refuse to have it happen to me. It was a tragedy—pure and simple. It's not an incident that has any sort of criminal element to it at all."

"And Donna's death?" asked Burton.

"Donna's death could be a total coincidence, as far as we know. It might not have anything whatsoever to do with Sally's death."

Burton gave him a doubtful look.

Roger said, "Maybe Donna interrupted a robbery in progress."

"At first glance, nothing appears to be ransacked or out of order."

Roger impatiently waved his hand. "It's not *my* job to speculate. It's *your* job to figure out who did it and bring the perpetrator to justice."

Burton grunted. I thought it showed admirable restraint that he didn't fire back at him. It was clear, however, that Burton wasn't exactly Roger's number one fan.

"Now, if you'll excuse me, I have a busy schedule today."

Burton nodded. "I know where to reach you if I have additional questions."

Roger looked displeased by the notion of Burton reaching out. He left quickly, glancing around him as he left to ensure no one had spotted him speaking with the police chief.

Chapter Thirteen

Grayson came back over to us. "That looked like quite the conversation there."

"None of this is on the record," said Burton in a very absent, automatic voice. He sighed. "Looks like this case is going to be a complicated one."

He was called away again by other police officers and gave us a hasty goodbye.

Grayson gave me a rueful look. "Sorry about dragging you into this. I never dreamed you'd be discovering a second body this week."

I waved my hand dismissively. "It's okay. I'm glad you weren't by yourself."

Grayson looked at his watch. "I thought we'd be over here longer, speaking with Donna. Is it too close to time for you to head to work, or can we grab some breakfast somewhere?"

I had the feeling Grayson also wanted to find out what Burton and Roger had been discussing. "Let's save the money and go to my house. After all my recent errand-running, my kitchen is pretty well-stocked. Besides, I'll need to pick up Fitz before I head to the library."

So that's where we ended up. Grayson put himself on egg duty, and I toasted some bread and started cutting up an avocado. A few minutes later, we were enjoying our breakfast with Fitz at our feet.

We chatted for a few minutes about what our upcoming days were looking like. Grayson's, as expected, had taken something of a detour with the discovery of Donna's body. He swallowed down some scrambled eggs and then said, "I hope you don't think I'm pushing you, but I'd love to hear what happened with Roger Young this morning. You know I'll never print anything that's off-the-record."

"Of course you won't." I gave him the rundown of Roger and Donna's past relationship, their college days, the friend who struggled with addiction, and that friend's untimely demise.

"Wow," said Grayson afterward.

"It's a lot, isn't it?"

Grayson nodded. "I've been reading Sally's book, but I'm going to have to pull an all-nighter tonight to finish it. From what I've seen so far, it looks like her book is based on the death of this college friend of Roger and Donna's."

"That's what it looks like. Sally wrote about a boy who was murdered and had his death blamed on an overdose."

Grayson shook his head. "Seems like Sally should have at least tried to alter the facts a little."

"Well, the name was changed and the details, I'm guessing. If she hadn't, she'd have been opening herself and her publisher up to potential lawsuits. Of course, when I was reading the book, I had no idea it was based on a true story." I paused. "I guess we still don't know that it *is* based on a true story."

Grayson said, "That's the thing, isn't it? Maybe Sally just wanted to throw Donna and Roger under the bus. The two of them could have been telling the truth, and it was *Sally* who was the one who was distorting the facts."

I considered this. "That could certainly be the way it played out. But if that were the case, there's got to be a good reason for Sally to want revenge on Donna and Roger."

"You said Roger was insistent Sally wasn't in their friend group, right? Could she have harbored some bad feelings about that?"

I shrugged. "Maybe. But if Donna and Roger ignored her attempts to befriend them, would Sally still care that much, years later? They didn't seem to have anything at all in common. Plus, Sally appeared to be more of an introvert. I can't picture her dying to be friends with anyone."

"True."

We finished up our breakfast, still thinking things over.

Grayson asked, "What did Roger say about what happened after they discovered Alan's body in the bathroom?"

"Roger said that he and Donna were very upset by it, and Alan's family was devastated. I got the impression that the reason it wasn't something he talked about was because he genuinely didn't think he and Donna had done anything wrong."

Grayson said, "You don't think Roger and Donna covered up the fact it happened at Donna's house?"

"I think there *was* some covering up, but it was mostly to prevent themselves from being included in any campus gossip. From what Roger said, they called the police right away, and the police came over to Donna's house."

"I did skip ahead in the book a little." He gave me a crooked grin that always made my heart give an extra beat. "I know that's cheating."

"I think it spoils some great books, but sometimes readers need shortcuts."

He looked relieved that he wasn't somehow violating any unspoken library rules. "Good. Anyway, when I was looking ahead, it looked to me as if the Sally character was a friend of the two killers. Do you think that means anything?"

"No idea. It could be Sally was just pretending to have that friendship she was looking for in college. Or it could mean that it was just a narrative device of some kind for Sally while she was writing her book."

Grayson asked, "Did Roger say what Sally was doing there when Alan died?"

"He thought it had something to do with the fact she'd been tutoring Donna. Roger figured Sally had walked in and misinterpreted what she was seeing."

"What *was* she seeing?" asked Grayson.

"I guess it must have been the scene in the bathroom—Alan being discovered, the way the scene looked with needles and drugs, that kind of thing."

Grayson took a sip of his coffee. Then he said, "What kind of vibes was Roger putting off?"

"Vibes?" I thought about it. "He was coming across as a pretty crummy person. I wasn't very inclined to vote for him anyway, and now I'm sure he doesn't have my vote."

Grayson looked interested. "I love hearing how public figures act in their private lives. It sounds like Roger isn't as nice as he seems on the campaign trail."

"Yeah, I think that's safe to say. He was condescending and downright rude to Burton. He acted almost as if he thought his campaign was more important than a murder investigation. Of course, to him, it definitely is. But he should have thought about how it was going to look to others."

Grayson nodded. "There's no way to make that type of selfishness look good."

"On the other hand, to be fair, he must have been feeling totally panicked. Here he was, on the scene of a murder. Something from his past, something he never wanted to come to light, was potentially being exposed. The last thing he'd want was a connection with a murder in both the past and the present."

Grayson mulled this over. "One thing struck me just now. We agree Roger had a motive for murdering Donna, right?"

"Absolutely. From the argument I heard between them in the stacks, Roger was very worried about Donna keeping quiet. Even in the silence of the library, Donna's voice was rising as her stress level went up. He must have been feeling pretty desperate to make sure she kept her mouth shut."

Grayson asked, "But you said Donna mentioned *she* was worried *Roger* was spilling the beans."

"Right. I'm guessing her concern was not about the overdose. I mean, neither she nor Roger would have wanted that to be common knowledge because it's the kind of thing that raises a lot of questions. But it wasn't as if they were at *fault* if their friend had an accidental overdose while they were around. That's what makes me think that Donna and Roger were concerned about having what *really* happened that night come to light."

Grayson said, "And, keeping the book in mind, that meant Donna and Roger were worried that the fact they murdered their friend, Alan, might come out."

"Right," I said again.

"Okay. So, if Roger went over to Donna's house early this morning and murdered her while she was in the yard gardening, why did he return to the scene? Wouldn't a guilty person know to keep away?"

We thought about this for a few moments. I said slowly, "Maybe Roger accidentally left something incriminating at Donna's house, and he came back to retrieve it."

"That's a possibility," admitted Grayson.

"Or maybe he's one of those people who likes to see the aftermath. I've read about those types of criminals. They return to the scene of the crime as if they're drawn there."

"I've heard that, too. Although it seems unlikely because he was so concerned about being seen. Or . . . maybe Roger didn't know anything about Donna's death and wasn't involved in any way," said Grayson.

"You think he was actually there to speak with Donna about a campaign event?" I asked with surprise.

Grayson snorted. "No. Like you said, that sounds like a total cover story. But maybe he'd gone over to Donna's house to warn her again to keep quiet. To persuade her to forget about what happened in the past. Maybe he even thought it might be worth his while to pay her off so his campaign wouldn't suffer."

I said slowly, "Then, by the time he saw all the emergency vehicles and realized what happened, it was too late for Roger to leave without being noticed. That could definitely be a possibility."

I glanced at my watch and grimaced. "Sorry, but we're going to have to wrap this up. I've got to get over to the library."

Grayson cleaned up the kitchen while I corralled Fitz into his carrier and grabbed my lunch out of the fridge for later.

He gave me a light kiss. "Thanks for inviting me over. I hope your day goes well. Better than it started out, especially."

I gave him a tight hug. "Yours, too."

When I got to the library, I spotted Luna in the children's area and waved her over. I wanted something to distract me from what I'd seen earlier, and Luna was just the person to do that. "So?" I asked with a grin. "How did the video game night go?"

Luna broke into an answering smile. "Ann, you wouldn't believe it. My mom took to Minecraft like she was made for it. She asked Jeremy a slew of questions at first and had a little trouble figuring out how to move around with the controller. But after that, she started building things."

"Hey, that's awesome! And the evening of fun was brought to her by Jeremy," I said. "That must really have helped her think kindlier of him."

Luna snorted. "I'd say. Mostly because Jeremy ended up having to leave his game over at our house so Mom could keep playing it. And, boy, did she keep playing it. I got up last night to get a glass of water and my mother was still in front of the computer at two o'clock in the morning!"

I said dryly, "I noticed she didn't come with you to the library this morning."

"Nope! She was in bed when I left the house. Who knows how long she was up? Anyway, she had an amazing time. And she invited Jeremy back over to play the game with her after work today."

I must have looked a little distracted because Luna suddenly gave me an analytical look. "Are you okay? Did something happen this morning? Everything with Grayson okay?"

I nodded. "Grayson is fine. But something did happen." I filled her in.

Luna shook her head, looking dismayed. "I can't believe it. This week has been crazy. That poor woman. I guess she must have known a little too much somehow. That can be a really dangerous thing. Did you get the sense the police were making progress?"

"I'm thinking Donna's death means there was a setback to their investigation." I shrugged. "Maybe there will be some more physical evidence on the scene today. The killer could be getting sloppy."

Luna shivered. "It seems really creepy. You feel you should be totally safe in your own backyard, you know? Poor Donna was out there working in her garden. I bet it didn't cross her mind that she was in any kind of danger."

"She probably didn't know what hit her," I said. "I guess that's a blessing. She had earbuds in, and I guess was listening to music. She wouldn't have heard someone approaching her."

"It makes it sound like whoever is behind this is getting desperate," said Luna, eyes flashing.

I nodded. "Well, they've got a lot to lose. They've murdered once and might be feeling like they got away with it. Maybe that made them feel bolder about taking out anyone they think might know too much."

Luna was about to say something else when she glanced over at the children's section. "Better run," she said in a rush. "Looks like a parent is standing at my desk."

With that, she scampered off, leaving me with my thoughts and a solicitous Fitz to keep me company.

Chapter Fourteen

The next four days went by in a much quieter vein. No bodies were found, no arguments overheard, and the library was running smoothly in every way.

I was just wrapping up a technology day at the library with the help of Timothy, a teen and loyal library patron who volunteered to get community service hours. The tech days were some of the most popular events the library hosted with people coming in with all sorts of electronic devices with all sorts of problems. Many of them were user errors, but it was great to help patrons sort out their issues and be able to use their devices again.

As Timothy and I were about to leave the community room at the end of the event, we saw an elderly lady approach us. She was carrying a tote bag.

"Lois?" I asked. "Is your laptop giving you any problems?" The last tech day we hosted, Lois brought in a brand-new laptop, which we helped her set up in every way possible.

Lois's bright-blue eyes beamed at us. "Not a bit. You two are geniuses."

Timothy blushed a little but looked pleased. "Wish that were true," he mumbled.

"It *is* true. I can't tell you how much time you both saved me. Not to mention the headaches I'd have had trying to figure out how to get that laptop up and running." She reached into the tote bag and pulled out a couple of round tins. "I made some of my world-famous chocolate chip cookies in gratitude."

Timothy's eyes lit up, and he eagerly reached for one tin. I smiled and took the other one.

"Go ahead," urged Lois. "Try one."

And, after putting a soft, chocolate-packed cookie in my mouth, I knew immediately why Lois said they were world famous. They were lightly crispy on the outside, chewy on the inside, and had a lovely buttery taste to them.

"Lois, these are amazing!" I said.

Timothy was so impressed by the cookies that he moved to eat another one, which made Lois chuckle. Finally, Timothy said, "There are different disciplines to be a genius in. I hereby name Lois a genius baker."

After visiting for another minute or two and hearing Lois say how much she was enjoying having video chats with her grandchildren on the other side of the country, I took my tin and headed over to the reference desk.

There I saw Wilson, looking around for me.

"Everything okay?" I asked. Wilson had too much of an air of mission and purpose for me to think he was looking for a chat.

"Hmm? Oh, yes. Everything is fine. The only thing is, I just found out that Sally Simmons's funeral service is in about an hour."

My heart sank a little as I realized Wilson was likely going to ask me to attend the service on behalf of the library. It wasn't the first time he'd done such a thing. In fact, he'd gotten quite fond of giving me impromptu assignments of all sorts.

"Is it?" I asked carelessly as I placed my notes about *Don Quixote* inside the book.

"Yes. And, unfortunately, I have another engagement this afternoon. A library board meeting. I do feel someone from the library should be there, especially since Sally passed away on the premises. I think it would be remiss for no one to attend."

I quickly glanced down at what I was wearing. Fortunately, I'd chosen a very muted outfit that morning and was in gray slacks and a cream-colored blouse.

Wilson cleared his throat. "I think your attire is completely acceptable for a funeral service. You understand why I couldn't ask Luna."

We glanced over toward the children's section to see Luna wearing bright-pink tights, a sky-blue skirt, and a green and purple top.

I nodded. "She could send the wrong message," I said dryly. "Unless it's a celebration of life service."

My last words were said in a hopeful way. Celebrations of life were generally much more pleasant to attend.

But Wilson was shaking his head. "My understanding is that this is a standard, graveside affair. I appreciate your stepping in." He looked at his watch. "You might want to take your lunch break now. I'm not sure if there'll be a reception after the service or not."

And with that, he headed quickly back to his office and hopped immediately on the phone.

I hopped on the phone immediately, too. Only I was calling Grayson.

"Hey there. I'm guessing you're planning on attending Sally's service today," I said.

There was a lot of noise in the background, so I could tell Grayson was at the newspaper office. It was usually something of a chaotic environment there with the sales staff garnering advertising, the photographer and reporter getting ready to head out on assignment, and all sorts of chatter going on.

"That's right. But you're working this afternoon, right?"

I said, "Well, I was. Wilson recruited me to represent the library at the service, though. I thought I'd see if you could swing by and pick me up."

"Sure," said Grayson. "See you in about forty-minutes."

Less than an hour later, Grayson and I were at the cemetery. It was a beautiful graveyard with old oaks forming canopies overhead. Some tombstones were well over a hundred years old. It had been bright and sunny that morning when I'd headed to work, but now the clouds had rolled in and set the stage for a fairly gloomy service.

As if he could read my mind, Grayson said, "It's very funeral-esque, isn't it?"

"It sure is."

There weren't many cars around or people in attendance. Grayson parallel parked on one of the interior roads and then looked over at the stray figures under the tent near the grave.

"I wish there were more people here," said Grayson with a sigh. "It's usually easier for me not to stand out." He glanced around again. "Unfortunately, most of the people milling around seem to be from the press."

There were indeed a few cameramen stationed a discreet distance away with their cameras trained on the mourners. There were also some snazzily dressed young women and men who didn't appear to be local.

"I know what you mean about wishing there were more people here. Well, we'll just sit near the back and give Steve our condolences at the end of the service."

"Steve? Is that Sally's boyfriend?" asked Grayson.

"Brother, actually. I'm assuming he's here. And I'm guessing the older couple are Sally's parents."

I felt my heart go out to them immediately. The couple were older-middle-aged and looked faded and exhausted. I couldn't imagine how hard the last week had been for them emotionally. No one expects to outlive their children. I also felt a sense of discomfort, almost as if I were trespassing at a private moment. I felt a small twinge of irritation at Wilson for forcing me to be here.

We were still in the car. "Which one is Steve?" asked Grayson.

I gestured briefly to the tall, blond young man. Then I looked closer. "I'm a little surprised to see Jason Hill here. He's the one who was Sally's ex-boyfriend. I know *I* feel awkward being here—I can only imagine what Jason must be feeling."

We got out of the car and headed quietly over to the gathering. No one was really speaking. Some crows were loudly cawing some yards away, and they were the only sound I could hear except for the far-off drone of an airplane.

The service started a few moments later and was just as quiet as the moments before the funeral had been. A very elderly pastor read some scripture. Then Jason rose to read a eulogy he'd printed out for himself. The eulogy was striking only because of the lack of any real personal information or insight into Sally. It was mainly full of generalities and phrases like "very promising writer," and "great big sister." But then, I figured, perhaps Sally had been just as much a mystery to Steve as she'd been to everyone else.

Burton was in attendance, as I'd expected. He was not gathered underneath the funeral home tent but was standing off to the side near to where the cameramen were. He had his dress uniform on and looked solemn.

Zelda had shown up a few minutes late, an expression of grim duty on her face as she plopped into a folding chair. Grayson and I shared a look. We hadn't expected to see Zelda there.

After about twenty minutes, the ceremony was over. "Ashes to ashes, dust to dust," intoned the pastor.

I was relieved it had drawn to a close. But then I saw Steve and his parents were walking away toward a parked car.

The minister said, "The family would like to invite all those in attendance to meet with them at a reception at the church hall."

There were murmurings among everyone attending. I had the feeling that most people felt like I did—that they had planned on offering their condolences after the service and heading out.

"Guess we're going to the church hall," said Grayson quietly. "Unless you need to get back to the library?"

I shook my head. "Wilson would want me to touch base with the family. Let's go to the reception."

The church hall was a cavernous space with minimal decoration and a scratched-up wood floor. The church had set up a long table filled with various casseroles and sandwiches. Unfortunately, it looked as though they'd planned for a much bigger group of people. The cornucopia of food threw the sparse attendance into sharp relief.

I looked immediately for the family but saw they were sitting at a table with the minister and already had plates.

"We'll need to wait until after they've finished eating," I said.

"Let's get ourselves a plate of food," suggested Grayson.

"I've already eaten lunch because Wilson and I weren't sure if there was going to be a reception. But I could get myself a snack," I said.

The snack options were limited, which is how I ended up with a motley assortment of ham biscuits, macaroni and cheese, and carrot sticks on my plate.

Grayson had apparently *not* eaten lunch because his own plate was heaped with fried chicken, green beans, broccoli casserole, and mixed fruit.

We sat down at a folding table topped with a white tablecloth. Moments later, a scratchy voice announced, "I'll sit down with you two."

I knew the owner of the voice before I even looked up. Zelda had quite the cigarette-smoking habit, and it had consequently ruined her voice. She was wearing black from her head to her toes, and it set off her henna-colored hair in a startling manner. She plopped down in the folding chair next to us and looked at her plate of food with dissatisfaction.

"Greasy food," Zelda muttered.

I smiled at her and changed the subject. I'd known from past conversations with Zelda that if I allowed her to, she'd end up complaining for fifteen or more minutes. "It was nice of you to come to Sally's service," I said. "Did you know her?"

Zelda shrugged. "From the library. I'd wave at her, and she'd wave back when I was shelving books. Wish I hadn't gotten to the service late today."

Grayson said, "I'm sure no one noticed."

Zelda beamed at him. Grayson was definitely a favorite of hers. For one thing, he was doing some volunteering for the homeowner association. Thus far, I had managed to escape the tentacles of the HOA, but Zelda continued trying to rope me in.

She said, "Couldn't get away from the repair shop. As soon as I was ready to head out the door, a slew of customers came in. It was madness."

I still had a tough time picturing Zelda in a customer-facing job. Her grim features rarely creased in a smile. But she was relentlessly organized and very reliable—two traits the car repair shop desperately needed.

Zelda stabbed at her fried chicken with a knife and fork instead of picking it up. She seemed entirely dissatisfied with the contents of her plate. Finally, pushing the plate away with a tsk, she said, "Wanted to speak to the family. Do you know who they are?"

I gestured briefly across the room. "They're at the table with the minister. The young man is her brother. I'm assuming the older couple are Sally's parents."

Zelda frowned even more than she already had. "Then who is that guy?"

Zelda had no unwillingness to point and point she did. Right at Jason Hill. Jason, seeming to feel our gaze on him, turned and looked startled at the sight of Zelda pointing directly at him.

Chapter Fifteen

I said, "That's Jason Hill. He was dating Sally for a long while."

Zelda finally put her finger down and grunted. "Okay. Well, I saw them together a lot."

"Did you?" Grayson asked. "Did Jason come by the library to see Sally?"

"Once or twice he did. But I saw them out together at the farm stand, too. Sally would help out."

Zelda thought hard a couple more moments. "Actually, I saw that guy with her, too, once. The one you said is her brother. He came into the library and was looking around everywhere. I thought he was casing the place to rob it later, so I had words with him." She sniffed.

I could imagine that Zelda most certainly had. If Fitz was the library cat, Zelda was its guard dog. She was zealously protective of the librarians' time and the building itself. Steve Simmons had probably gotten an earful.

"Did he say why he was there?" asked Grayson. He seemed to suppress his own smile at the thought of Zelda taking on Steve.

"He told me he was looking for his sister and gave me a description after I asked for it. I led him to her and then stuck around for a moment to make sure he hadn't lied to me, and he wasn't some sort of stalker or something." Zelda's fierce expression promised trouble for the young man if he had been.

I asked, "Was Sally happy to see him?"

"She certainly was not. She was in the middle of working on her book and didn't want to have anything to do with him. Sally said something like, 'I told you I'm not giving you a cent.' That's how I could tell he was being a pest. Then he started pressuring her. He said something like, 'You can afford it.' And Sally was shaking her head and telling him to go."

Grayson asked, "Did Steve go?"

Zelda shook her head, henna-colored hair flying. She looked most displeased at the memory. "He kept wheedling. So I marched right up to him and told him he was in the quiet section, and he needed to leave immediately or I was going to call security."

I smiled. This would be the non-existent security. The librarians handled the few incidents that came up. "Did that work?"

Zelda looked satisfied. "He left right away."

"You also mentioned you'd seen Jason and Sally together. Did you think they made a good couple?" asked Grayson.

The question was more nosy than pleasant conversation, and Zelda picked up on this. She wagged her finger at him. "You're doing some reporting, aren't you?"

He grinned unapologetically at her. "I'm just trying to come up with a profile of Sally. It's very helpful to know a little about her relationships."

Zelda nodded thoughtfully. I could tell she liked the idea of contributing to a potential article. "Well, it was hard to tell. Sally didn't seem to be the kind of person who wore her emotions on her sleeve."

That was very true. Sally seemed to have only one expression as far as I'd been able to tell: guarded. But then, if she'd been writing a book based on true crime, perhaps she was smart to be watching her back. Unfortunately, it hadn't worked.

Zelda seemed as if she very much wanted to be helpful. "But that Jason, you could tell he was crazy about her. He only had eyes for her. I didn't feel like she was all that interested in him. He'd reach out for her hand, and she'd pull it away. That kind of thing."

Grayson said, "That doesn't sound too surprising. Sally ended up breaking up with him not too long ago."

"Figures," said Zelda. She looked at her watch and narrowed her heavily outlined eyes. "I need to get out of here and get back to the shop. They won't mind if I go up there and talk to them."

And with that, Zelda picked up her plate of food, tossed it in a nearby large rubber trashcan, and plodded off to the table where Sally's family sat with the minister.

I said, "I always feel as if a tremendous burden has lifted when Zelda leaves. I know that's terrible to say."

"She's a character," said Grayson with a grin.

"You handle her a lot better than I do."

"Maybe that's because you have to deal with her more than I do. She doesn't volunteer at the newspaper office. Thankfully." Grayson looked thoughtful. "So why do you think Sally stuck around with Jason for as long as she did? Do you think she just enjoyed avoiding conflict and didn't want to break up with him?"

"I think she might have been using him. I believe Jason suspects it, too. That Sally was living with Jason so he could support her while she wrote her book. From what I understand, she didn't send out a book proposal."

Grayson asked, "What do you mean?"

"Just that Sally didn't get paid an advance for the book until she'd already finished it. She queried a completed manuscript and not a book proposal. So, to write her book as many hours a day as she did, she needed some sort of support."

Grayson nodded. "That must have been hard on Jason. No one likes feeling used." He glanced over to where Zelda was walking away from the family's table, having done her duty. "I wonder why she didn't just move in with her brother or her parents while she wrote the book."

"Well, according to what Zelda was saying, her brother wouldn't have been a good choice. Steve had mentioned right after Sally's death that he needed a loan, but he made it sound as if it wasn't a big deal. Zelda makes it sounds as if he was pretty desperate for cash. Maybe Steve would have taken her in, but she might have thought it was just easier to stick with Jason. As for her parents, my understanding from what I've read online is that they live out of state."

"Got it." Grayson looked away and added, "Looks like Steve is making the rounds. Heads-up."

Sure enough, Sally's brother was approaching our table. We gave him a smile.

"Hey there," he said, smiling back at us. He was looking dapper in what looked like a new suit. "I really appreciate you coming."

I said, "I'm here on behalf of the entire library. We're so sorry again about your sister."

Steve nodded. "I appreciate that."

He was looking at Grayson as if he wasn't completely sure who he was. Before I could introduce him, Grayson introduced himself. He said, "I'm actually representing the newspaper. I'm writing up a profile on Sally to show she was more than just a victim. I want to present a well-rounded view on her."

I wasn't sure how Steve was going to take that, but he looked pleased. "That's great. I know the local paper will do a better job with that. I've been mostly turning down interview requests from the national media because I don't think they'll do Sally justice. They were going to turn the whole thing into a crime show. You know: famous author is murdered. That kind of thing."

Grayson smiled at him. "I totally understand that. It sounds like you two had a good childhood together. You must have been close."

There was no way Grayson could have discerned that from Steve's vague eulogy. But it made Steve looked even more pleased.

"We were," said Steve. "Sally and I had a great childhood. She was really fun-loving back then. We'd play in the creek, looking for salamanders and crawfish. Sally was always very creative, even back then. She'd make up all sorts of games for us to play. We spent all day in the woods."

He was doing a better job eulogizing Sally now than he had previously. Maybe he was one of those people who didn't enjoy public speaking.

"It's good to hear you had such a carefree childhood," said Grayson.

Steve sighed. "Yes. Sally wasn't always the way she'd been recently. She was very different when she was young. Before she went off to college." He turned to me. "What did you make of Sally?"

He seemed genuinely curious, so I thought a few moments before I formulated a response. "To me, she seemed to be very studious. Serious, I suppose. And introverted . . . which isn't a bad thing," I hastened to add. "I'm introverted, myself."

Steve nodded, agreeing with my assessment. "Sally wasn't always like that, like I said. I can't help but think something happened to her in college to make her change. Something bad. She might have done better if she'd just attended Whitby College instead of going away to school."

"Why do you think that?" asked Grayson.

"There were just too many students there. Sally was the kind of person who'd have done better in a smaller environment with fewer students. She'd have liked to develop a relationship with her professors, for instance. I remember when she came back home from school on a break. I could see she was already in that shell she built around herself. I think she just got lost in the crowd at the university."

"But she'd wanted to go away for school originally?" I asked.

"That's right. Sally was all excited at the thought of going to Charlotte. She said she was tired of being in a small town and wanted the experience of a big city and a big school. She showed me the college brochures listing all the organizations and clubs and ways to connect."

"Did she do a good job connecting with others?" asked Grayson.

Steve shook his head. "I don't think so. The only thing I heard that she was doing there was tutoring. Sally had always been a great student, so that didn't surprise me. But I thought it was kind of sad that she hadn't joined all the clubs she'd talked about. I mean, I didn't think she was going to be the type to join a sorority or anything, but I thought she'd at least join a service organization or something."

"Did you ask her if something was wrong?" I asked.

"Yep. I figured something wasn't right when she came home one time on break. But she told me to back off. That she didn't want to talk about it. I wondered if maybe she'd had a bad relationship at school. A bad breakup or something. I mean, college was supposed to be a fun time. But the opposite was true for Sally. Plus, I overheard my folks talking about her grades. They took a tumble at one point. She was able to get them back up again, but I remember it took my parents by surprise."

"How are they doing?" asked Grayson in a quiet voice. "With processing Sally's death, I mean."

Steve shook his head. "I don't think it's really hit them yet. It's like they're stunned or something. That's why I'm coming around and greeting everybody. It's really hard on them. They were so proud of Sally and her book." He sighed. "I've still got to read the book."

I said slowly, "From what I understand, parts of Sally's story might be based on actual events. Events that were set from the time she was in college. I was wondering if those events might have created the change in Sally's behavior that you were talking about."

Steve raised his eyebrows. "That would help explain a lot. I know it's not exactly a cheerful book, right?"

"It's about a murder that happened during college. And a cover-up," I said.

"Well, that would sure help explain things," said Steve. "Maybe she thought writing the book would help her get rid of some of those feelings she was carrying around with her. I wonder how much of it was based on the truth and how much Sally made up."

Grayson said, "On a slightly different topic, I was surprised to see Jason here. I understood he was pretty upset at Sally for breaking up with him."

"Yeah. I'm surprised to see him here, too. It makes me sort of upset, actually. Jason was really mad at her. I guess he thought she'd been using him. And she probably was. But Sally did what she needed to do to survive. She could have moved in with Mom and Dad, but they live in Georgia now, and Sally liked it here in Whitby. Now I'm thinking it would have been better for her if she'd just left. She might still be alive."

Grayson asked, "Was Jason supportive of Sally's writing?"

"Oh, definitely. At first, anyway. He acted like he was totally devoted to her. He didn't ask her to do much, especially considering he had a farm and could have used the help. He was the first one to cheer when she told us she'd gotten a publishing contract. But it wasn't like the two of them were married. Sally didn't owe Jason anything." He paused. "I still think Jason might have had something to do with Sally's death." He glanced up at Grayson. "This is off-the-record, right?"

"Of course."

Steve continued, "Jason and Sally weren't really getting along even before Sally broke up with him. Sally just put up with Jason and never argued. That was because of her situation, of course."

"Do you know what Jason was upset about?" I asked. "You were saying he didn't ask a lot of her, and he was supportive."

Steve nodded. "Which is true. But he was also pretty particular about things. Jason didn't ask Sally to do anything but to pick up after herself. The only problem was that Sally wasn't exactly the neatest person in the world. Even when she was a kid, I remember our mom fussing at her because she'd throw her stuff all over the place as soon as she came in from school. She'd leave dishes in the sink and papers everywhere. Laundry on the floor. You know, that kind of thing."

"And it drove Jason crazy?" asked Grayson.

"Right. He was pretty much a neat freak. Not in a bad way, though. I mean, I was on Jason's side. It seemed like the least Sally could do was to pick up after herself, even if she wasn't contributing in any other way." Steve shrugged. "But that's just who Sally was. I think he really got on her nerves when he asked her to clean up. I remember I was over there for supper one time. Jason had cooked the meal, full of fresh vegetables from the farm. But Sally's stuff was all over the table. He asked her to clean the table off so we could sit there."

"And that bothered Sally?" I asked.

"Yeah. I could tell it did. Like I said, she wasn't going to argue about anything because of the fact he was putting her up. But she had this hard look in her eyes. I had the feeling that she was going to be dumping Jason as soon as she had the chance."

Steve looked across the room and frowned. "I don't think cops should go to funerals. What's he even doing here? Burton didn't know Sally. This is supposed to be for Sally's friends and family."

Grayson said, "I don't think it's unusual for them to be at a funeral after a suspicious death. I'm sure he's hoping to get information to help him solve the case."

"Well, it makes me feel uncomfortable," said Steve. "It's just another reminder that Sally's death wasn't a natural one. Plus, the cops have been questioning me like they think *I'm* a suspect. I had nothing to do with Sally's death. Why would I? I was her brother. Sally and I always got along great."

I remembered what Zelda had said about the argument in the library. Was Zelda exaggerating when she said Sally and her brother had argued over money? Was it just a normal sibling dispute? Or was there something more there?

Steve continued, "They've even been asking me questions about this other murder."

"Donna Price?" I asked.

He nodded, looking irritated. "I know the cops think the two deaths are connected, but I'm really scratching my head over that. They asked me what I was doing when that woman died, and I told them I didn't even know who Donna *was*. They had to show me a picture and then I told them I'd seen her around town. But when she apparently died, I was getting ready for work. It wasn't much of an alibi, but why would I kill somebody I didn't even know? For that matter, why would I kill *anybody*?"

It seemed like a rhetorical question, so Grayson and I just sat quietly.

Steve looked down. "I just keep thinking about what Sally had ahead of her and how it was all cut off. Maybe I should have said something like that in my eulogy, but I had a hard time writing it. I'm not somebody who spends a lot of time doing public speaking or anything. But now I keep thinking about how Sally found all this success and was on her way to getting more. She didn't like doing interviews on camera, but she'd just agreed to do one with one of those morning shows."

"Was she excited about it?" asked Grayson.

Steve shook his head. "I was more excited about it than she was. I thought it was going to be a great way for her to get even more readers and more buzz for her book. But she was more resigned than anything else. I couldn't figure out why she wasn't jumping up and down over all the success she was having. It makes more sense if the book was a true story. Or if parts of it were true."

His eyes narrowed as he looked across the room again. "I seriously can't believe Jason is here. Like I said, he definitely had a motive to murder Sally. Isn't that the way it goes with cop shows? It's always the husband or the boyfriend who did it. I know it really bothered him when she left him. But that's life, you know?" He shrugged. "The cops should spend their time looking at *him*. I loved Sally. I know the cops probably say that Sally had a lot of money and I killed her for it. But I'd never have done anything to harm her. Or this Donna, whoever she was."

Steve gave another sigh. "Anyway, I've talked your ear off. I'd better go speak to some other people. Thanks for coming to the service."

Chapter Sixteen

Grayson and I left another ten minutes later. I said, "That was a pretty eventful service."

He nodded. "Exactly. It was all off-the-record, of course, but we got a fuller picture of what's going on. Even Zelda was useful."

"For once," I said with a chuckle.

"Sounds like Steve was a little more desperate for cash than we realized. That doesn't mean he killed Sally, but it certainly makes his motive stronger."

"Absolutely," I said. "And for his part, Steve was very down on Jason. I wonder if that was because he needed to shift blame from himself, or whether he genuinely thought he could be involved in his sister's death?"

"Maybe a little of both," said Grayson. He glanced over at me in the passenger seat. "On a totally different topic, film club is tomorrow, isn't it?"

I nodded. "Are you going to make it?"

"Is Lars coming?" he asked with interest. Then he quickly said, "Not that I wouldn't want to come anyway, to see you."

A smile pulled at my lips. "I see how it is," I said teasingly.

Grayson chuckled. "It's even more fun to go with friends there."

Lars was one of Grayson's quieter friends but was someone I'd really warmed to. He was quiet, a big reader, and enjoyed off-beat movies. It made him a perfect candidate for the film club that the library sponsored every month. Grayson had pulled

Lars along with him during a recent event and Lars had been very interested. But then, we had some great club members.

"As a matter of fact, Lars picked the film this month," I said with a smile.

Grayson's eyes widened. "No way! Is it one of those weird arthouse films that he likes so much?"

"Well, it's an arthouse film, for sure. It's one of the more mainstream ones, but it's still pretty crazy. I'm going to let you find out when you get there. I think Lars wanted the title to be a surprise."

Grayson snorted. "Probably because nobody would show up if it was something too bizarre."

"Well, it couldn't be anything *too* strange because we have Mona there. And sometimes Wilson. Mona's a good sport, but if things get too crazy, she'll pick up her knitting and start working on it. It had to be something to appeal to almost everybody to be a film club pick."

"I'm definitely going now," said Grayson with a grin. "It's a date."

I walked into the library and settled in at the circulation desk as soon as I saw the number of patrons waiting to check out materials. It looked like it was an all-hands-on-deck situation. There were a lot of little kids in there with their moms and dads checking out picture books. That always made me smile. Sometimes I stepped in to sub for Luna during storytime and loved the whole process.

After a while, Wilson walked over, fresh from his board meeting. "How did it go?" he asked.

"The service? It went well. I spoke with Sally's brother and told him everyone in the library was very sorry for his loss."

Wilson nodded, looking pleased. "Thanks for doing that. I'd have gone myself if I hadn't had the meeting."

Mona spotted Wilson and came up from the reading area in front of the fireplace. Luna often brought her to work with her in the mornings to give Mona the chance to get out of the house. She and Wilson could usually catch lunch together, although I had the feeling Wilson had a working lunch today with the trustees. He was usually fond of ordering in lunch for them.

Wilson, always rather starchy, wasn't much in for public displays of affection. So it meant a lot when he reached over and brushed Mona's cheek with his lips. She flushed happily.

"I'm guessing you had lunch with the trustees," Mona said.

He nodded. "But I put aside some food for you." He held up a bag I hadn't noticed. "If you haven't already eaten lunch, that is—I know it's pretty late."

Mona looked pleased. "That was thoughtful of you! No, I haven't eaten yet, although I brought some leftovers. I can just eat those tonight. Will you sit with me outside while I eat?"

There was a little sitting area out on the grounds of the library with benches and tables, an umbrella, and even a fountain. I was fond of the breakroom, but it was also nice to sit outside sometimes and get a little vitamin D. Plus, the landscaper we used did a great job out there with the knockout rose bushes and some gorgeous azaleas.

Wilson glanced at his watch and looked over at his office as if mentally calculating the amount of work he needed to accomplish. "I think I can manage that." He smiled at her.

Mona said, "Great! I can also tell you all about my plans to have a card night. Jeremy, Luna and I are going to play hearts and we want you to be the fourth. I would include you with our video game night, but I'm not sure you'd enjoy that."

Wilson looked as if he weren't entirely sure he'd enjoy the card night either, and I hid a smile. He gave me a rueful look and meekly accompanied Mona outside for her lunch.

The next morning, I headed back again to the library in the pouring rain. Still, if it had to rain, it was better that it happened then and not during the funeral service.

Rainy days at the library could mean we'd be completely quiet—or teeming with people. I never could figure out which would happen. Fitz knew exactly how to spend rainy days at the library. He found either someone's lap or a quiet spot in the building and fell into a contented sleep. I only wished I could do the same. There was something about the tap of the rain on the roof and the dim light filtering through the windows that made me want to go back home and climb into bed.

I was working at the reference desk when I saw Liv Nelson come in and head toward me.

"Hi there," I said. "Sorry to make you come out in the rain. I could have emailed the list of attorneys to you."

She shook her head. "Oh, I wanted to get out anyway, despite the weather. I've been feeling really restless lately and thought it might be a good idea to just run errands. Take my mind off things." She had a hollowed look in her eyes, but it was a look I'd noticed before with her. I didn't know Liv well, but it seemed like she might have gone through some tough times in her life.

I printed out the list and handed it to her. "Do you still feel as if the police are considering you a suspect? Because you said Sally had plagiarized your book?"

Liv gave me a sharp look as if she hadn't expected me to ask her more questions about the book. "Why do you ask?"

I was going to just say I hoped the police were giving her a break. But I felt a little miffed that Liv had said Sally had copied her book idea. Especially since it was now clear that the book had been based on actual events. Tragic ones, from Sally's own experience.

I quietly said, "It's just that some more information has been uncovered. It looks as if Sally's book was inspired by actual events."

Liv took in a quick breath. Then she looked away as if trying to figure out what she was going to say next. I guess she figured she couldn't lie anymore. She slumped a little. "Okay. It wasn't that Sally stole the idea from me. I guess I felt sort of embarrassed by the real reason we had bad blood between us. I'd been dating Jason. You know, Sally's boyfriend."

I frowned. "You mean after Sally broke up with him?"

Liv shook her head. "Before. He and I went to Whitby College together. Jason had been a business major when I started dating him and was just realizing it wasn't for him when I came on the scene. That's when he switched over to agriculture. We only dated for a little while before we came to the mutual decision that we'd be better off as friends. You know how some relationships are like that."

I did indeed know that. Before Grayson came along, having dates turning into friends was something I usually encountered.

It seemed for a while like I couldn't hit it off romantically with anyone.

"So you didn't mind when Jason started dating Sally, I guess."

Liv shrugged. "I was happy for him. I thought 'good for him.' I missed seeing Jason as much as I had because we really *were* friends. But I understood that when he got a new girl-friend, she probably wouldn't be crazy about having him hang out with an old girlfriend. Besides, it was a really busy time for me as a teaching assistant and student. I had tons of projects to write and to grade."

I said, "I know you've spent a lot of time in the library to get your stuff done."

"Exactly. I saw Sally here, of course, and I'd say hi to her. But she was really cold to me."

I had to wonder if Liv was exaggerating Sally's reaction to her. Most likely, it was just Sally's usual reserve that Liv had seen.

Liv said, "Anyway, I knew the police would make a big deal over the fact that I used to date Jason, so I didn't say anything about it."

"Why did the police think of you as a suspect?"

Liv looked a bit flustered. I didn't think I was getting the full story from her. She said, "Oh, Sally and I had a little spat out downtown not long ago. I guess somebody must have men-tioned that to the police."

"A spat?"

Liv nodded. "Jason had told me that Sally had broken up with him. He seemed really devastated about it. He felt like she'd been using him to write her book and then broke up with him as soon as she got a check from the publisher." She shrugged. "I saw Sally out not long after that, and I couldn't help myself. I told her off. It was no big deal—I was just standing up for my friend."

"How did Sally react?" I asked curiously.

Liv shrugged. "She just stalked away. I was still flinging accusations at her back as she left." She gave a rueful smile.

"So when the police asked you about the argument, you told them it was because she'd plagiarized."

Liv flushed again. "It was a dumb thing to do. I just latched onto the first idea I had. I thought it would be worse to say that I'd been that close to Jason. Then they'd think I'd been jealous of Sally."

I wasn't totally sure her allegation of plagiarism was worse than admitting she'd dated Jason at one time.

"Nobody would have known about it at all if someone in town hadn't mentioned it. Whitby being Whitby, somebody in town had to squeal on me," said Liv.

I said, "I don't think you grew up in the area, did you?"

Liv shook her head. "Charlotte. But I loved going to undergrad here and decided to settle and continue here for grad school. It's always seemed like such a peaceful place. Until lately. I couldn't believe it when I heard about Sally." She looked down at the list of attorneys in her hand. "It would probably help if I had some sort of alibi for Donna's death. I'm sure the police are going to be speaking to me soon."

I figured they would be too, but I asked, "You think so?"

"Sure. If they thought I might be responsible for Sally's death, it's a short leap for me being a suspect for Donna's. But all I was doing was preparing to teach class and looking over my notes. That's not going to help the police get off my back." She hesitated. "Attorneys are pretty expensive. I wonder when I need to loop them in."

"I'm not sure," I said. "Maybe you should ask them."

Liv nodded. "Right. Makes sense."

"Have you thought anymore about who might have done this?" I asked.

"That's pretty much *all* I've been thinking about," said Liv ruefully. "It's been keeping me up at night. If the police could just figure out who's behind this, I wouldn't have to worry about lawyers. The person I've been thinking about the most is Roger. That's just because Donna died. Like I said, I didn't know Donna, but I did see the two of them huddled together when I was out in town."

This sounded very much like what I'd witnessed in the library. "They were just talking?" I thought about Roger and how important appearances were to him. I couldn't imagine he'd have been happy with Liv or anyone else witnessing an argument.

Liv said, "Well, Roger, since he is running for office, was looking all around and making sure no one was seeing them together. I got the impression that maybe they were an item."

"An affair?" This surprised me. I hadn't gotten that impression at all when I'd overheard the two of them. Plus, Roger had said they'd dated in college, but had broken it off shortly after Alan's death.

Liv shrugged. "Maybe. I don't know. It seemed to me like the two of them had a past together. Or maybe a present. I just overheard Roger being really insistent that their secret not slip out. I was coming up from behind him on the sidewalk and he couldn't see me. Donna was too wound up to care if I were there or not. I was thinking maybe they were having an affair that Roger was worried was going to come to light. He's married, after all."

I'd seen Roger's wife occasionally. She looked like the perfect candidate's wife. Her long, honey-colored hair was always perfect, as was her expertly applied makeup. She was often at his campaign events, although she hadn't been at the library event. She definitely didn't seem like the hothead Donna had been.

Liv was still mulling things over. "Of course, like I mentioned before, it could be Sally's brother Steve. Having Sally's money will definitely make his life easier for him. But I have no idea why he'd want to kill Donna." She sighed. "It's all such a mess. I used to think I wanted to live in Whitby, but now I'm thinking as soon as I graduate from grad school, I'm going to move away."

"I'm sorry to hear that," I said. "It's a great place to live."

"Yeah, but not with people gossiping. Even if the police catch whoever's behind these two murders, people are still going to wonder and talk. I'll never escape the local gossip. It's just the way small towns are." She glanced at her watch. "Well, I've talked your ear off enough today. I better head out. See you later, Ann. Thanks for the list of lawyers."

I took a quick glance at my own watch and realized it was time to set up for film club. In fact, Mona was already walking over to the community room. I'd gotten so caught up in my conversation with Liv that time had totally slipped by me.

I hurried over and unlocked the door with my key. "Sorry," I said to Mona. "I've lost track of time today. I'll have the chairs set up in a jiffy."

"I can help you out," said Mona with a smile.

It was sweet of Mona to offer, but she'd had some orthopedic surgery in the not-too-distant past and the last thing I wanted was something to happen to Luna's mom on my watch. "Thanks, Mona. I've got the chairs, though. You could help me out with the popcorn machine. If you know how to run it, anyway."

Mona looked pleased to be invited. "I've seen you do it gobs of times."

So Mona measured out the popcorn after I pulled out the machine and I hurriedly set up the folding chairs as she chatted about Wilson's interest in her seed library idea.

Lars was in the room just minutes later. Not only was he early, but he'd also dressed up for the occasion and was wearing khaki pants and a button-down shirt. Truth be told, he didn't look much like Lars at all. He was clutching a stack of papers which I gathered were his notes for the film. He gave me a somewhat nervous smile.

I smiled back at him. "Hi Lars. Have you met Mona yet?"

Mona and Lars introduced themselves and then Mona said, "I hear from Wilson that you might have a very eclectic selection for us today."

Lars looked even more nervous at the idea of the library director commenting on the choice of film. "Did he?"

I smiled at him. "Don't worry. Wilson was the one who selected *2001: a Space Odyssey* for his choice. It's not exactly the most traditional option out there. And this group is very open to watching different things."

Lars looked at Mona's kind, grandmotherly face as if he really hoped that were true.

"What's the name of the movie today?" she asked. "Maybe I've seen it before."

Lars cleared his throat. "It's *Being John Malkovich*."

"Hmm!" said Mona. "A documentary, is it?"

"Actually, no," said Lars, somewhat apologetically. "It's more of a fantasy film."

Mona's brow furrowed. "A fantasy documentary? Mercy. They'll mash together all sorts of genres now."

Lars appeared concerned that he'd left Mona with the wrong impression. "It's not really a documentary at all."

"No? But isn't John Malkovich an actor?"

Lars nodded. "He is, definitely. But it's not about him. Not really. It's a comedy."

Mona's furrows became deeper. "It's not a fantasy?"

Lars gave me a rather desperate look.

I threw him a life preserver. "It's one of those arthouse films that you really can't encapsulate, Mona. In fact, if Lars tries to, he might ruin the experience for you."

"I see," said Mona slowly. I saw her glance behind her to make absolutely sure her bag of knitting was there.

Lars helped me finish setting out the last row of chairs. He said in a low voice, "I hope this movie isn't going to fall absolutely flat. It's definitely not *E.T.*"

"Like I said, this group is open to new experiences." I tried to sound soothing and matter-of-fact, but Lars didn't look too sure.

Timothy, our teen film club member, came into the room. He grinned at Lars and me. "I hear we've got something cool in store today."

"We do," I said. I introduced Timothy and Lars, but it looked like they'd already met each other at the last meeting.

Timothy said, "Hey, Grayson was telling me that you're in IT."

I added, "Timothy volunteers for tech day here at the library."

"What do you do with computers?" asked Timothy.

Lars looked relieved that I hadn't immediately tried to recruit him to volunteer for tech day. "I'm a programmer. I do some pen testing, too."

I wasn't computer illiterate, but I had only recently understood that pen testers are authorized by large corporations to try to hack into their system and learn the security faults. Timothy apparently knew all about it.

"Really?" he said admiringly. "I'd love to do something like that one day."

"Is that what you're planning on studying in college?" asked Lars.

Timothy nodded. "That's a few years off, though. That's why I'm trying to get volunteer hours at the library—I thought it would be good for my applications."

"What kinds of issues do you come across on tech day?" asked Lars.

Timothy and I smiled at each other. He said, "Well, it could be anything. But usually, it's a really simple problem to fix. The best part is that it only takes a few minutes to fix, and then the person is just so totally happy. They're grinning ear to ear. It's like we made their day."

I saw a flicker of interest in Lars's eyes. "That's actually very cool. It must give you both a sense of satisfaction."

I smiled at him. "It definitely does. That's why I'm in this job. I mean, I'm not saying that sometimes working with the public or trying to help someone who doesn't totally understand what they're doing isn't tricky. But it's worth it."

Timothy looked at me. "Those world-famous cookies from Lois."

"Exactly!" I saw Lars looked confused and said by way of explanation, "We have a patron who we helped with setting up her new laptop. As a matter of fact, Timothy actually helped her *buy* it a couple of weeks before that."

Timothy said modestly, "I just made sure she was getting something reliable that would fit her needs and didn't have a bunch of bells and whistles that she didn't need."

"She was so pleased that she brought us the best homemade cookies I've ever put in my mouth."

Lars now looked even more thoughtful. "That's great." He hesitated. "I just don't know if I'll always be available when you're having your tech days. I don't want to bail on you or anything."

I opened my eyes wide. "Are you thinking about helping us out?"

Lars clearly didn't want to commit. "I'd like to sometimes. It's just that the kind of work I'm doing right now isn't something I find particularly rewarding. I mean, it pays the bills and I like my coworkers and that kind of thing. It's also pretty flexible work."

I couldn't tell if Lars was trying to convince me that he had a good job or was trying to convince himself.

Timothy said, "So, you're thinking you might find more satisfaction through volunteering."

Lars smiled back at him. "I think I might."

"I'll email you some information about it and you can look it over," I said. The room had been rapidly filling up while we were chatting. "I'd better run get the film ready to load. Then I'll give you a quick introduction and let you take the floor to talk about today's pick."

Lars looked a little nervous again but gave me a quick nod.

But his nerves were relieved a few minutes later when everyone gave him a round of applause after he announced the selection.

George, a film club regular who had a typewriter repair shop on the square, said, "Man, I've had this movie on my watchlist for ages. Glad I'm finally going to get the chance to see it."

Mona, thankfully, had not yet pulled her knitting out of her bag. I kept my fingers crossed that the film would keep her engaged enough to actually watch it.

I turned the lights off and settled into a chair. A few moments later, someone slipped in beside me. I turned and saw it was Grayson.

"Sorry," he whispered. "Running a little late."

I gave his hand a squeeze, happy he was there and spending the next couple of hours with me.

About halfway through, I glanced around the room to see what everyone's reactions were so far. Mona was still knitting-free, although she had a puzzled frown on her face. It was a film that wasn't for every viewer. It was definitely edgy, but she seemed like she was handling it all right. Timothy was clearly enjoying the movie and laughed out loud several times, as did George. It looked like it would be considered a success. I was glad—not that we hadn't aired duds before. I'd definitely screened a film or two that the group just didn't really go for. But with Lars so new to the group, I was glad that his pick was well-received.

There were plenty of questions, of course, for this very unusual film. Lars fielded them well and also pulled out some trivia for the movie that he'd found online. Afterwards, the club lingered, catching up with each other and chatting.

"What's the rest of your afternoon look like?" asked Grayson.

I looked at my watch. "I'm actually scheduled to leave in a few minutes. So I'll clean up in here, lock up the room, and then head out. I was thinking about picking up some fresh vegetables at the farm stand on the way home."

Grayson raised his eyebrows. "Jason Hill's farm stand?"

"That would be the one," I said with a grin.

"Is that on the way home for you?"

"It's a minor detour. Fitz will be happy to see some different scenery. And I thought vegetables would be great for supper tonight. Do you want to come with me?"

Grayson looked very much as if he'd like to. "Unfortunately, I have a staff meeting with the team. Do you think I could join you for dinner, though? Maybe hear what you found out from Jason?"

"If I'm able to find out anything at all. But supper would be great." Sally's ex-boyfriend didn't seem to be the most forthcoming, but I hoped maybe he'd be curious about Donna's death. Maybe that would spark a conversation.

Grayson lent me a hand with putting the community room back to rights. Then he and Jason chatted on the way out to the parking lot. I finished up a couple more things on the reference desk, then put them away. I packed Fitz up into his carrier and we took off.

Chapter Seventeen

Jason's farm stand wasn't too far off the beaten path. Whitby was the kind of town that still had family farms close to the town center. His stand had been around for years. He even had a refrigerator for the beans he'd picked and his fresh eggs. He also had a variety of different jams and jellies, honey, and a great selection of salty pickles.

Jason was wearing bib overalls, and a brimmed hat. He looked like he'd been working in his fields before heading over to the farm stand. His mud-splotched overalls lent some authenticity to the scene.

The farm stand was a nice draw, and Jason had done a great job setting it up. The small building was made of wood and held shelves with baskets tilted toward customers so they could see the bounty from the street. He always kept a nice supply of local foods there, and I spotted baked goods today.

Jason nodded at me when I came up. "Hi there, Ann."

I set Fitz's carrier on the ground next to me, ensuring he didn't stay in a hot car. "Hi, Jason."

"Who've you got there?" asked Jason, peering at the carrier.

"Oh, this is Fitz. You might have heard of him—he's the Whitby Library cat."

While Jason stooped down and stuck his fingers in Fitz's crate to say hi, I picked out a motley assortment of veggies, making sure I got enough for both Grayson and me. Luckily, Jason had a bumper crop with tomatoes, cucumbers, various peppers, lots of beans, and some cantaloupe. I also got a jar of honey which I liked putting in my coffee in the mornings as a sweetener. My allergies always seemed to be better when I used it.

"Looks like you found some good stuff," said Jason with a smile.

"Oh, just wanting something good for salads. Easy meals, you know." I paused. "I see you've got some baked goods today, too."

"Sure do. Emma Baker has been baking up a storm. I'm very partial to her sourdough bread if you'd like to try it."

I loved getting fresh bread when I had the chance. I certainly wasn't one to bake it, myself. It seemed sort of fiddly having to feed the dough with a starter. I checked the price of Emma's bread and found it was a lot less expensive than I was concerned it might be. I put a loaf over at the cash register.

Jason smiled at me. "I think you'll enjoy it."

"How are things going?" I asked as I put the bags of produce down in front of a scale.

Jason looked a little guarded. "I guess it's going as well as could be expected. With everything going on, you know." He paused. "I wanted to thank you, by the way. It was nice of you and the library to put on that event for Sally. I don't think I ever said that."

I smiled at him. "Thanks. We like to support folks in the community. It's what the library is all about."

I thought it was generous for Jason to think about Sally's event. He had every reason to feel bitter about her success and the attention she'd garnered.

He must have read my mind, because he said, "I've been thinking about everything with Sally. I've been feeling a lot more philosophical about it, I guess. I thought the worst of Sally at first, and I don't feel very good about that. I immediately assumed she was using me until she was able to make it as a writer. But after talking with some of my friends, I've realized maybe Sally wasn't really using me. Maybe she was just so focused on her book and making it perfect that she just didn't have time to examine our relationship and the problems we had."

"That makes a lot of sense," I said. "This book, from what I understand of it, might not have been the easiest story for her to tell, either. She could have been so absorbed in the process that she couldn't really think about anything else."

Jason nodded, warming to his topic and seemingly relieved that I agreed. "Then, when she'd finally finished writing the book and it was out of her hands and at the publisher, she finally had the time to take a closer look at our relationship. That's when she probably realized the two of us just weren't going to work out. Anyway, I wouldn't have wanted to be part of a relationship that wasn't working, either."

"That's true," I said. "It would be terrible to be with someone who wasn't happy. I think it would be very stressful."

Jason continued, "I love the freedom I have in my life right now. If I'd been stuck with somebody who was unhappy, it would be miserable. Like being trapped. So, in some ways, I feel like Sally did me a favor."

I pulled out my wallet to pay for my purchases. I casually asked, "Was the friend you were talking to Liv?"

He brightened at the mention of her name. "That's right. I guess you know her from the library. I know she's in there all the time. She's been a great friend to me. Liv's another person where the relationship between us just didn't work out. But instead, I gained a friend. We've known each other since college."

"You met in class?" I asked.

He nodded. "There was a general education class that we were both in that was required for graduation. It was music appreciation or something like that." He smiled at the memory. "Not that either of us really appreciated much of the music we were studying. It was a lot of stuff we didn't care much for." His smile faded a little, and he said in a more serious tone, "I really respect Liv because she had a rough time as a teen, and then ended up coming through it all. It makes me realize we're all a lot stronger than we think we are."

"I'm sorry to hear that. I didn't know Liv had a tough time growing up." It could explain the solemn expression I frequently saw on her face.

Jason said, "When her older brother died, her whole family broke apart. Of course, it was awful for her parents to lose a child. Her father left the family, her mother drank all the time. Liv had to pretty much take care of herself, and she was still just a kid."

"That's awful." I hadn't had the easiest time as a kid either, and stories like Liv's always resonated with me. But at least I'd had my great aunt to take care of me . . . and she'd done a great job. It sounded as if Liv hadn't been so lucky.

"Yeah, but she had a happy ending, didn't she? She's amazing. She somehow focused everything on her studies, made fantastic grades, got scholarships for school, did great in college. Now she's in grad school. I think that's why I wanted to date her in the first place—I was just so impressed by her." He paused.

"She mentioned you were helping her out by researching good lawyers. I just hope nothing is going to happen to derail all the progress she's made in her life. The cops don't think she had anything to do with this other death, do they?"

I shook my head. "I'm afraid I don't have any idea. I'm sure they're just trying to ensure they're getting as much information as they possibly can to solve the cases." I paused. "Did you know Donna at all?"

Jason shook his head. "Not really. She came by the farm stand sometimes, but she wasn't really one to talk to me. She was usually in a hurry. I hear the police think the two murders are connected."

"That's what I understand."

Jason pressed his lips together in annoyance. "I'm sure the police will be back by to speak with me, then. I know people in Whitby think I had something to do with Sally's death. I know I have a temper, and sometimes I don't do a great job at keeping a handle on my emotions. But whenever I raised my voice at Sally, it was because I was hurt. What people don't understand is that I really cared for Sally. I'd never have done anything to harm her."

I remembered what Zelda had said at the funeral reception about Jason having an argument with Sally not long before her death. "Did you have much contact with Sally before she died?"

Jason gave me a sharp look as he handed me the bags of produce. "No. When she broke up with me, we really didn't have anything to do with each other after that."

I hesitated. I wanted to bring up what Zelda had said to see how he responded to it. But I knew I was out here with no one else around, too, and I didn't want to be stupid.

Then a car pulled into the small parking area in front of the stand. A middle-aged woman sat in the car for a moment, texting. I figured if Jason was actually the murderer, he wasn't going to be brazen enough to take me out in front of the woman.

I said, "Just a heads-up that there was a witness to an argument you had with Sally shortly before her death."

Jason looked startled for a moment, then resigned. "I don't know why I thought no one heard that. I know exactly how small towns are."

"I thought the police might question you about it. So I thought I'd give you some advance warning." As if my only motive was to be helpful.

"I appreciate that," said Jason. "I didn't want to say anything about it because I worried the police would misunderstand and think that I was guilty. The truth is that I did talk to Sally, and it definitely started out as an argument. My feelings were hurt, and my heart was hurting, too. So I told her what was on my mind."

"Did she say anything in her own defense?"

Jason shook his head. "She wasn't defensive at all, actually. She heard me out and told me she felt bad about how things had ended between us. It ended up being this really constructive conversation. Sally told me she regretted not telling me earlier that she didn't think it was going to work out between us. She said she didn't have a good explanation for it, but that it had to do with her being so focused on her book. Writing the book was this very cathartic experience for her, she said."

"Did she say anything else about the book?" I asked. I was still hoping maybe she'd told Jason more about how the story was inspired by true events. It would also have been nice to know how Sally felt about what happened during school and how she knew about it to begin with.

He shook his head, his mind clearly still back at that day in the library. "She didn't talk about the book at all. She just focused on our relationship. She said that she hated she was so selfish. That I deserved better." He smiled. "I felt so much better after I'd talked to her. It's like I knew at that moment that I could move forward—maybe find someone else to date. The hurt sort of evaporated. That's why I had no motive to murder Sally, no matter what the cops think. I was putting my relationship with Sally behind me."

I glanced quickly at the middle-aged woman in the car. Fortunately, she seemed to take her time with that text message, but I knew my opportunity to ask Jason more about this was limited. He'd be helping that woman with her produce before long.

"Do you have any more thoughts on who did all this?" I asked.

Jason pressed his lips together and then said, "Not really, although if I figure out who killed Sally, he better watch out. I still think it could have been Sally's brother Steve. He's going to end up directly profiting from Sally's death. He's never had two cents to rub together, so I know it's going to be a windfall for him."

"Did you get a sense of what Sally made from the publishers as an advance?"

Jason said, "I know it was six figures. And I know she was supposed to make royalties after she earned out the advance. Anyway, it's a lot of money. I'm sure Steve is happy about that." He paused. "Did Steve and this Donna know each other?"

"I'm not sure," I said.

"Maybe Donna knew something, you know. Maybe that's how the two deaths are related to each other. Donna could have spotted Steve at the library before Sally died. Other than that, I can't think of a reason he'd have killed Donna, too."

Jason's cell phone made a chirping sound, and he quickly glanced at it, his face relaxing into something approaching a smile. He said a little shyly to me, "I've actually met someone else, as a matter of fact. I'm not sure if we're going to end up in a relationship, but I'm looking forward to seeing where it takes me."

"That's great!" I said, meaning it. That was probably the best way for Jason to move on.

He nodded, looking pleased. "Yeah. Her name is Tatum. Do you know her?"

I shook my head. I was sure in a town the size of Whitby that there was only one Tatum, and the name didn't ring a bell.

"A friend of mine suggested I should start going back to church again," said Jason with a small shrug. "I'd sort of gotten out of the habit. Farming will take over your life if you let it. So I headed over a couple of weeks ago. I thought it might also help me get over some of this anger I felt toward Sally. I mean, like I said, I'd mostly felt freed after that conversation with Sally in the library, but there was still this residual anger and hurt. I met Tatum at church, and we got to talking. Seems like she and I have a lot in common."

"She's a farmer, too?" I found this rather unlikely, but thought I'd ask.

The question made him laugh. "No. She's a CPA. I meant we have a lot in common in other ways. Similar interests, I guess. Anyway, things are looking up."

The middle-aged woman finally finished her epic text message and climbed out of her car with a couple of tote bags she apparently intended to fill with produce. Jason immediately snapped into professional mode, greeting her briskly and giving her an overview of what he had in stock.

"I'll see you later," I said to him, stepping away with Fitz in tow.

"Thanks for coming by."

Chapter Eighteen

It was quiet at the library when Fitz and I arrived. It wasn't a storytime day, so there was just a single family in the children's section, looking for books. It was too early for students to be there. I saw Mona and Linus in the sitting area by the fireplace, Mona knitting and Linus reading. They both lifted a hand to wave at me.

I got settled behind the reference desk and Fitz got settled into a sunbeam in the reference area. I didn't have anything immediately pressing for work. Later, I needed to select new materials for the library collection and weed out some older ones. That could all wait.

I knew the first thing I wanted to do was to learn more about Liv Nelson. There was clearly more to her than met the eye. She'd taken the police on a wild goose chase when she'd claimed Sally stole her book idea. She'd acted as if she were just a regular grad student and didn't mention she'd dated Jason prior to his dating Sally. And she'd been very interested in my putting together a list of attorneys. None of those were particularly suspect, but when taken together with what Jason was saying about Liv's horrible childhood . . . I wanted to check it out. Liv gave me the impression of someone who was stuck in her sadness and couldn't find her way out of it. She was so striking-looking with her black hair and brown eyes. But you could tell there were things in her past that weighed deeply on her.

It took a bit of digging. But then I found a reference to Olivia Nelson, a survivor of Alan Nelson in a brief obituary.

More digging uncovered the fact that this was the same Alan whom Donna had referred to. The one who'd died on the floor of her bathroom in college.

I sat still, staring at the screen. Then I dug some more online. This time I wanted to find out more about Alan Nelson. Luckily, he'd been on social media before his untimely death in college. There were some pictures of him with friends, grinning a cheerful grin with his arms around them. Despite what had been said about Alan's drug use, he didn't seem to be under the influence in any of them—not even the ones where he'd been tagged by other people.

There'd been quite a few memorial posts by his friends. From what they said, he'd been fun-loving, warm, and a good friend. Although people often turned dead peers into saints, it made me wonder if Donna and Roger had been telling the truth about Alan and his alleged overdose. What if there was something more to it? What if they'd covered up the real way he'd died? And what if Alan's younger sister, Liv, was out to get revenge?

I knew I didn't have any actual evidence. I felt like I needed to get in touch with Burton to let him know what I'd found out about Liv. They might well have gotten there before me, but I didn't want to withhold anything that could help them out, if they hadn't. I gave Burton a call. He didn't answer, so I left a somewhat rambling message telling him what I'd found out and asking him to give me a call.

Then I got back to work on updating our collections. Weeding out old or out-of-date books from our collection wasn't my favorite part of the job, but it needed to be done. I tackled it first. Sometimes it was better for me to just get unpleasant tasks done first thing. That way I had a smug feeling the rest of the day.

I headed to the stacks with a list I'd started on the items that weren't checked out very often. That was one sign a book wasn't particularly useful to the community. I'd also checked to make sure that the books, if needed, were still available through our interlibrary loan program so that patrons could access the books if they really needed to.

I could hear Zelda's voice from the nonfiction section and bit back a sigh. It sounded like she might be on her soapbox. She could be very protective of the librarians' time, even though we'd told her it was our job to help the patrons, no matter what their request was, and even if it meant interrupting what we'd been working on.

As I got closer, though, I could tell it wasn't Zelda's usual soliloquy. She was telling someone about opportunities at the auto repair garage where she worked. Out of curiosity, I walked around a shelf of books to see who she was talking to. My eyes widened when I saw Steve Simmons, Sally's brother, standing there.

Now Zelda's heavily mascaraed eyes looked at me as if disapproving that I'd stepped away from my desk. "Can I help you, Ann?" she asked with a sniff.

"No, I'm just getting started with weeding the collection." I gave Steve a smile, hoping one of them would tell me what their conversation was about so that I wouldn't seem impossibly nosy.

"Hi, Ann," said Steve. "Zelda was just telling me they're really short-staffed at the garage where she works."

"We're *always* short-staffed," she corrected. "We can't seem to get enough mechanics. It makes life very difficult for me on the phone. I have to tell people we're backed up and their vehicles won't be ready when they want them to be. It's incredibly inconvenient for our customers. And for me as the receptionist." Zelda's face indicated she was itching to step into the back of the shop and jump in to help.

I said, "I didn't realize you had experience as a mechanic, Steve."

He shook his head. "I don't. But Zelda was just telling me I could go to the community college and take some classes."

"Absolutely. They've got an automotive systems curriculum there. I helped another patron navigate the enrollment process there. You can end up with a lot of different certifications and a diploma."

Steve looked a little uncomfortable. "Are there a lot of prerequisite classes you have to take before you start with the cars? I dropped out of college before I really finished anything."

I said, "If you go with the diploma route, I think there is a prerequisite English and math requirement. But for the different certificates, you can jump right in. We can look at it if you'd like."

Zelda, for once, was looking pleased. So was Steve.

"Yeah, that would be great. I don't want to interrupt you from what you were doing, though," he said.

"Weeding books can always wait," I said quickly.

He smiled at me. "That would be great then. I keep feeling like I'm just going from one dead-end job to another." He paused, looking concerned. "I don't have the way to pay for classes right now, though. I mean, not until after probate."

I said, "I can help you look up student loan information. And give you a hand with applying, if you'd like."

"You would?"

"I've done it lots of times for patrons. It's one of the regular requests I handle."

Then Steve followed me to the reference desk where we started the process. As we walked away, I could hear Zelda humming as she shelved books.

At the end of the day, I still hadn't heard back from Burton. I hoped there hadn't been some sort of setback that was holding him up. On the upside, maybe there had been some recent, helpful developments that he needed to explore.

I couldn't get Liv out of my mind. Not with knowing what I did about her past and the fact that her brother was the one who'd died that night with Donna and Roger present. I'd already looked online to see where she lived. I wondered if Grayson would go with me to pay a visit and ask her a couple of questions.

I put Fitz in his carrier and drove home absently, still thinking about Liv. As soon as I was home, I got Fitz settled with his dinner and some fresh water and gave Grayson a call.

"Hey," he said. "Everything okay?"

Maybe he could feel the frisson of energy on the other side of the line. I was definitely keyed up, feeling as if maybe a few answers might be ahead.

"Everything is fine, except I have a lead."

Grayson sounded keyed up now, himself. "On the case? What happened?"

I told him what I'd learned from Jason about Liv's past and what I'd found out online. "I was wondering if we could go over to her house and talk with her. I've left Burton a message, but I haven't heard from him yet. What do you think?"

I could tell Grayson was grinning on the other end. "You're going to ask a reporter what he thinks about approaching a suspect with new information?"

I chuckled. "Dumb question."

"You're at home now?" Hearing my confirmation, he said, "I'll be there in five minutes."

Five minutes later, I was climbing into Grayson's car. I put in Liv's address, which I'd found online, and routed us over there.

Grayson glanced across at me as he drove. "Are you thinking this is the end of the case? That Liv killed Donna and Sally for revenge?"

"I'm not really sure what it means. It could be something Burton and the state police were already aware of, and it's just new information for me. Or maybe Liv went after Donna and Sally, just like you said—that she realized what had happened after reading Sally's book."

Grayson nodded, eyes on the road. "I just finished Sally's book last night. I saw it outlined a coverup. So you're thinking that Liv thought her brother's death was straightforward when it happened, right? That she believed he'd gotten involved with drugs once he was in school and suffered an overdose?"

"That's what I'm thinking. She would have still been barely in high school then and not on the scene at all. When Liv read

Sally's book, she must have known Alan's death was more than a drug overdose, if what she was reading was true. Liv must have recognized the scenario Sally wrote about and that it was her brother who was represented."

Grayson said, "How did Roger and Donna get the drug paraphernalia, then? Were they the ones who were using, and they used their own supplies to fake the overdose?"

"I'm not sure if the drugs were theirs or not. Maybe Roger was a user or knew a fraternity brother who had drugs on hand. Or it could be that Alan did actually have a drug problem but never overdosed."

"In the book, the Alan character was arguing with Roger and Donna. Donna stomped off to the bathroom to get away, but he followed her in there. Then Roger shoved Alan, and he hit his head on the porcelain sink. Sally never put herself on the scene there," said Grayson.

"I figured Liv realized that Sally must have been there to have written about it with such detail. Maybe Liv thought Sally was also involved and had felt so guilty over Alan's death that she decided to write about it . . . just keeping herself out of the story."

Grayson pulled the car onto the curb, on the other side of the street. Liv's house was a small brick ranch with lots of trees in the front yard. We walked to the front door. I hesitated. This was always the worst part—ringing the doorbell. Fortunately, Grayson had no problem with this and immediately pushed the bell.

I felt a sense of unease as we waited. Grayson must have noticed, because he reached out and held my hand, giving my fingers a squeeze. "It's okay," he said in a quiet voice. "She won't be able to take both of us on, if we find out she's the murderer."

I squeezed his hand back. He was right, of course. Even if she was armed, surely she wouldn't be able to subdue both of us. And murdering us in her own home would certainly present her with a problem.

There was a rustling of the curtains by the front door, and then I saw Liv's face, grim, peering out at us. She looked briefly surprised, then as if she wasn't entirely sure she wanted to open the door at all. Then I saw her drop the curtain, seemingly to move to the door.

Chapter Nineteen

Liv's expression was wary, although she had a faint smile on her face. "Ann? What's going on?"

She looked at Grayson. "It's Grayson, right?"

He nodded.

I took a deep breath and said, "Liv, there was something I found out when I was at the library. I wanted to ask you about it because it's been on my mind all day."

The faint smile disappeared, and that wary look intensified. She glanced around at the neighbors' houses and then said slowly, "Maybe you should come inside."

Part of me wanted to stay outside on her doorstep where Grayson and I could quickly bolt to his car. I glanced over at Grayson, and he gave me a small nod. With that, we followed Liv inside.

Liv's house was plainly decorated with sparse furnishings, befitting the home of a student. She led us back into her kitchen at the back of the house where there was a rickety table with a few brightly colored chairs around it. "Can I get you something to drink?" she asked.

Grayson and I shook our heads and sat down. He looked at me as if to tell me to go ahead.

I decided to come right out with it. Liv clearly wasn't happy about us being there and despite the offer of drinks, she knew this wasn't a social visit. "I spoke with Jason earlier today. He mentioned that the two of you had been friends for a while. He talked a little about your past."

Liv tilted her head to one side. "What did he say about it?"

"Not much. Just that you'd had a hard time after your brother died. That your family had, understandably, gone through a rough spot."

Liv gave a short laugh. "Well, that's one way of putting it. Basically, everything fell totally apart. I've heard losing a child is the worst thing that could happen to a marriage, and it definitely was for my parents'. My dad ended up leaving us to fend for ourselves. My mother started drinking to drown her sorrows the best way she could. I was so desperate to get out of there that I started studying as much as I could. For one thing, studying was a good distraction from everything happening in my life. For another, I figured scholarships were the only way I could further my education. My dad sure wasn't going to pay for it." Her voice was bitter.

Grayson said gently, "You and your brother were close?"

"Well, there was a four-year age difference there, so in some ways we weren't as close as we could have been if we'd been closer in age. But I totally idolized him. I looked up to him like he was the most amazing person I knew." Liv gave another abrupt laugh.

I said slowly, "When Jason told me your story, it sounded a little familiar. When I went back to the library, I did some digging."

She shrugged. "I'm sure there was plenty of stuff written about it."

"Actually, there wasn't. But I learned that your brother was Alan Nelson. That he'd died of a drug overdose in college."

"*Alleged* overdose," said Liv quickly.

I nodded. "Exactly. I found quite a few parallels between what Sally had written about in her book and your brother's death. I wondered how much of Sally's story was true."

Liv slumped in her chair, looking down at the table. "That's what I'd wondered, too. Maybe I should have looped you in, Ann, as soon as I found out. It looks like you've already learned plenty about it. This was why I wanted to get that list of lawyers. I knew the cops wouldn't believe what I'd been trying to do. All I wanted was just to speak with Sally. It seemed like she was the one who knew what actually happened the night Alan died."

"Were you able to talk to her?" asked Grayson.

Liv shook her head. "No. I didn't get the chance before she died." She rubbed her forehead absently with her hand. "That was so frustrating. I knew she'd be able to tell me what actually happened that night. What she was doing there, what she'd seen, and whether what she wrote in her book was fictionalized or the truth."

"What did you think when you read the book?" I asked.

Liv blew out a long sigh. "Well, when I first started reading, I was mostly just interested in the book because it was a local author with a bestseller. But as I got into the story, I realized how much it sounded like what had happened to Alan . . . all except the part where a simulated drug overdose was used as a coverup for manslaughter. I read her book all in one sitting."

Grayson said, "You never told the police about the similarities?"

"Of course not. They'd have thought I was suspect number one. That's probably what the two of you think, too. Look, I never laid a finger on Sally. She was key to me figuring out what really happened to my brother. I was totally frustrated when I found out she was gone. And, much as I suddenly suspected Donna and Roger of being involved with my brother's death, I didn't have any real evidence. Not unless Sally had talked with me and confirmed it. As far as I knew, Sally could have made the whole thing up."

Grayson said, "So you had nothing to do with the deaths. But you also *knew* who might have a motive to kill Sally and, later, Donna."

Liv nodded, looking pale.

There was suddenly the sound of a faint knocking sound near the front of the house.

Chapter Twenty

Liv turned even paler. She whispered, "No one ever comes to visit me here. I hang out with friends in town. I almost didn't answer the door when you two knocked. That *was* a knock on the door, wasn't it?"

Grayson said in a low voice, "That's what it sounded like."

This was followed by a louder, more persistent knock.

"Liv, if you're innocent of these murders, then you're in danger, too," I said. I knew if the crimes were connected to Alan Nelson's death, and it wasn't Liv or Donna . . . I had the feeling I knew who was at the door.

Liv murmured, "Whoever it is has got to be stopped. This needs to be over. You two hide and record what happens." She headed to the door, our pleas for her to stay back falling on deaf ears.

Grayson grabbed a kitchen knife, and I pulled out a frying pan. We hid behind the wall leading into the living room.

I fumbled with my phone, setting it to record. Grayson, seeing me, did the same in case one of our phones didn't record well.

"What are you doing here?" demanded Liv.

We heard a rough voice say, "Let me in." Despite the frantic sound of it, I recognized it right away. It was Roger Young.

"Why do you have a knife?"

Grayson and I looked at each other grimly.

I heard the front door being pushed shut with a bang that made me jump.

"Why do you think?" asked Roger. "I know who you are. I don't know why I didn't recognize you earlier. Alan brought you along for family weekend."

Liv said in a shaky voice, "We'd have had more of those if you hadn't done what you did. I read the book, Roger. I know you were the one who shoved Alan in the bathroom. You killed him."

"It was an accident," hissed Roger.

"Were Sally's and Donna's death accidents, too?"

Roger seemed determined to ignore that. "Alan was shoving me, too. I wasn't the one who started things. He's the one who showed up out of the blue. It could just as easily have been me that died and not Alan."

"But strangely enough, it wasn't," said Liv in a sarcastic tone. "What was the argument even about? In the book, it was because Alan didn't like the way you were treating Donna. He was trying to be a good friend to her."

"He was trying to get in everybody else's business," grated Roger. "If Donna wasn't happy with our relationship, she was free to move on."

"The worst part was the cover-up," said Liv. "Was Alan even on drugs at all? I'm thinking he didn't have the money for heroin. That's pretty pricey for a college kid. But *you* did. Did you use your own supply and paraphernalia to make it look like Alan overdosed?"

Roger was silent.

"That's what I thought. It just killed my parents, you know. My father left and my mother drank constantly. They both lost their jobs because of what happened and when they lost their jobs, I lost all my security. The whole trajectory of my life changed," said Liv heatedly. "I'd been on-track for my future and really had to scramble because all of my support systems were gone: my brother, father, and mother."

Roger said in an icy voice, "That's precisely why I covered things up. That trajectory you're talking about. I'd been on a good one and had no intention of messing up my future, especially over Alan Nelson. He was dead anyway, Liv. Nothing was going to change that. I hadn't acted with any sort of malicious intent. There was no reason for me to get charged with anything just because of an accident. Not over a loser like Alan."

I heard an incensed gasp from Liv. I peered just barely around the edge of the wall in time to see her smash a glass vase over Roger's head. Grayson and I came running over as Liv knocked the knife out of Roger's hand, and I scooped it up.

Roger's eyes were enormous. He scrambled off the floor and made for the door. He was stopped as Grayson tackled him, and Liv and I grabbed onto his arms.

Which was when my phone rang with Burton's return call.

Chapter Twenty-One

The three of us were able to fashion makeshift restraints for Roger out of some duct tape Liv found and some clothesline until Burton came by.

He did, quickly, with the state police in tow. He looked somber as he came in, shaking his head at Roger.

Roger quickly said, "It's my word against theirs, Burton. I simply stopped by to see Liv since she was the sister of an old friend of mine."

Roger's imperious tone annoyed me. I said, "Oh, didn't Grayson and I mention? We taped your little conversation with Liv."

Roger slumped slightly, but I could tell his mind was racing. "If I cooperate, would it be a reduced sentence?"

Burton said, "That would be up to the courts. But I would definitely put in a word that you offered up information. Are you wanting to make a confession?"

Roger silently considered this, then nodded.

"Okay. I'm going to inform you of your rights. Then you can tell us what happened with these three deaths."

"Three?"

Burton nodded and said grimly, "My understanding is there was one from long ago, too. Later, you're going to sign the confession at the station."

The fight seemed to suddenly go out of Roger. I could tell he was still trying to think of a way out of all this—to get back to where he was yesterday, Candidate Roger Young. But he clearly realized he was cornered. Burton read him his rights.

Roger took a deep breath. The state police had voice recorders and Burton was poised with his pencil stub over his notebook again. "Okay." He paused. "I'm not even sure where to begin."

Burton said dryly, "I guess that's the way it goes when you've killed a lot. Let's start with when you realized what Sally's book was about. I'm thinking you lied about that, too. You must have read it."

"Like I said, I don't have time to read books right now. I read a review on the book online and saw that her plot seemed to shadow what had happened when I was in college. I looked online to see if I could find more information about the book. There was plenty of basic stuff online, but Sally hadn't done a lot of interviews. After some digging, though, I knew Sally had basically just written what had happened that night."

One of the state policemen interjected, "What was Sally doing there that night? I thought you weren't acquainted with her."

Roger gave a short laugh. "I *wasn't* acquainted with her. I knew who she was, of course. But she was Donna's tutor. All I knew was that she seemed to hang around Donna a lot. Like she wanted to be friends. As if she had anything in common with us! I never knew she was there that night, but she obviously was. I'm guessing she came to the house, knocked on the door while we were arguing with Alan in the back, and let herself in. Donna must have had tutoring. She was always forgetting it."

Burton said, "So Sally went in and saw what happened. How did you end up in the bathroom with Alan? I'm assuming that part of Sally's story was accurate."

Roger narrowed his eyes, remembering. "Alan was mostly focused on yelling at me for the way he *thought* I was treating Donna. I always had the impression he had a crush on her. But then he started giving Donna a hard time. Alan told her he expected better from her. That she could find someone who really cared about her." The last was said in a sneer.

Burton waited for Roger to continue.

Roger sighed. "Donna burst into tears. She was always a pretty emotional person. She rushed off to the bathroom, and we followed her." He paused, brows drawn together as he remembered the night. "There was a bunch of yelling. Donna was upset and yelling at both of us to stop. Alan was telling me off. I was defending myself. There wasn't much space in that bathroom, and it was an older house." He set his chin stubbornly. "Alan shoved me first."

I could tell Burton wasn't very impressed with this excuse. He gestured for him to continue.

Roger said, "I shoved him back. Alan seemed like he tripped over one of the bathroom rugs or something. Anyway, he fell backwards. He hit his head on the sink." He pressed his lips together, remembering. "It made a terrible sound. I knew right away he was gone."

"In Sally's book, you came up with the idea to cover-up the way he'd died," said Burton. "But wasn't there a sign of the injury he'd sustained?"

"I didn't look very closely. But anyway, I figured it was something that could have happened with an overdose, too. He could have overdosed while in the bathroom and fallen over, hitting his head as he did. At any rate, the cops didn't seem to ask a lot of questions when they showed up. And the school didn't want it to look like anything but a natural death. So there wasn't a lot of digging going on." He shrugged. "I worried for a while that they *would* try to do an autopsy. Then they'd have been able to see that Alan wasn't a regular heroin user. But the school and the authorities were more concerned about keeping everything quiet."

Burton said, "How long after you read Sally's book before you murdered her? Was it immediate? Or did you have to plan it?"

Roger shrugged. "If I was going to do it, it needed to be done soon before people started asking a lot of questions. I knew it was going to be only a matter of time before someone made the connection that there had been a fatal overdose during the time Sally was in college."

I gave Burton an apologetic look because I wanted to ask a question. He nodded at me to go ahead. I said, "How did you know to find Sally in the library? Did you spend some time following her?"

Roger pressed his lips together in irritation. "I couldn't follow someone around like a stalker. I'm a political candidate."

Not anymore, he wasn't, I thought.

"Anyway, I read up on Sally. As much as I could, anyway. Like I said, she didn't seem to welcome the opportunity to do many interviews. The ones she did do, however, mentioned her writing routine. It was set in stone. Since the library is a public place, I figured it would be simpler to approach her there instead of at her home."

"Approach her," said Burton grimly. "You mean kill her."

"It was what I had to do."

Roger wasn't going to be owning up to any sense of guilt for these deaths. To him, he just did what he needed to do in order to survive. I felt a slight chill as I looked at him.

"And Donna Price?" asked Burton. "She clearly wasn't in a public place. Were you just desperate enough that you realized you needed to finish her off, regardless?"

"I wouldn't have said I was *desperate*. Again, it was just a means to an end. Donna was a loose cannon. She was spouting off her mouth too much and behaving recklessly. She called me at the campaign headquarters, asking to see me. She was approaching me out in public and demanding to know what had happened to Sally and how we could protect our secret. But the way she was acting, she was the one who was going to end up exposing us. I didn't have a choice."

Burton's face looked as if it were carved from stone. I could tell he didn't think much of Roger's excuse that he didn't have a choice. Roger, with his influence and affluence, had more choices than most people did.

In the interest of keeping the interview going, however, Burton continued without contesting him. "So you decided to silence Donna permanently. You went to her house. I'm guessing she wasn't expecting you."

Roger shook his head. "She wasn't. Although she certainly would have opened the door to me if I'd knocked. She was trying to get in contact with me all the time, like I said. I could tell people at the office were wondering who the woman who was calling me all the time was."

"But when you got to her house, you realized Donna was outside in the backyard. Out of view. That must have been a relief to you."

Roger shrugged again. "It made things easier. She never saw me coming."

Liv broke in, with a shaking voice. "And me? What about me?"

Roger gave her a look full of dislike. "After Donna's death, when I was out driving, I saw the police talking to you outside your house."

Burton raised an eyebrow. "But we could have been talking to Liv for any number of reasons."

"Of course," said Roger brusquely. "But I realized then that something had been bothering me about Liv. I'd seen her other times around town before all this started and thought I remembered her from somewhere. I couldn't remember when. Seeing the police talk to her made me start digging. I looked through some of the photo albums from my college years. Alan and I had been good friends, so there were plenty of pictures of us together. We were in the same fraternity. Then I noticed a few pictures from various family days at the school. Alan's sister looked a good deal like Liv."

"You've got quite a memory," said Burton wryly.

"It helps in politics to remember faces. I confirmed the fact by pulling up Alan's obituary and seeing the survivors there."

It was very much the process I'd taken to learn more about Liv. And obviously, Roger had reached the same conclusion.

Liv spoke again, her voice stronger and sounding angry now. "So you decided you'd get rid of me, too. Because I was someone who could make the connection between you and my brother's death."

Roger said coolly, "It was the next logical step."

I'd never been so glad that a person would not end up in public office.

Burton said, "So you came over here with a knife." His eyes landed on the knife, still on a nearby table. "I guess you were just getting increasingly desperate."

Roger, again, didn't seem to like the word *desperation* being applied to himself. He glared at Burton.

"It's a good thing you happened to have a crowd here," said Burton to Liv.

She smiled at Grayson and me. "Tell me about it."

Grayson said, "You were doing pretty well on your own, there, Liv. Nice moves with the glass vase."

Burton said, "What made the two of you show up here?"

Grayson nodded at me. "Ann figured out who Liv was. We originally thought she might be the one responsible for the deaths."

Liv said, "I totally get why you would have. I had plenty of motive. And, believe me, I've always wanted to kill whoever ruined my family."

Burton closed his notebook and stood up. "Well, you'll hopefully get a little peace now, Liv. The guy responsible is going to be put away in jail for a long time." He hauled Roger to his feet.

"Remember our deal," muttered Roger.

"I'll be sure to say how cooperative you were," said Burton. "Although with a couple of phone videos of what happened, I think the jury will find your confession isn't quite as impressive."

Burton and the state police officers left with Roger in tow.

I said, "Liv, we'll head out now, too. Are you sure you're okay? That was a pretty scary scene for a few minutes."

Liv nodded. Then she reached out and gave Grayson and me an impulsive hug. "Thanks to both of you, it didn't end up as bad as it could have been. I'm not sure if I'll be able to sleep tonight." She paused. "I may need you to help me come up with a new list this time, Ann. Maybe for therapists."

"Of course I can help out. I'll get started on that tomorrow."

Liv looked pleased. "Thanks. Everything that happened made me realize I hadn't worked through any of the feelings I had after Alan died. I haven't been able to put the breakup of my family and Alan's death into the past. I think it's probably time I talked things through with somebody."

A few minutes later, Grayson and I were back in his car again. I looked over at him. "Okay, that was absolutely not the way I thought our evening together was going to work out."

He reached over and gave me a quick hug. "Are *you* okay?"

I nodded, taking a deep breath. "I think so. Although I'm absolutely starving."

"Want to head over to Quittin' Time?"

It was one of the few affordable restaurants in town. I smiled at him. "That would be perfect."

And so we headed over there. It was a slow night at the restaurant, so we were able to relax over our food in relative quiet. We carefully avoided talk of what had happened, instead enjoying our burgers and fries. And a couple of beers, too.

The next morning, I was back at the library. Fitz was curled up in front of me on the reference desk as I opened up a box of new fiction arrivals for the library's collection.

I was frowning at a cover when Wilson came up.

"It's not another local author, is it?"

Wilson's voice was full of such trepidation that I couldn't help but smile. "It's not as if local authors make a habit of getting murdered."

Wilson sighed. "I suppose you're right. I'm just glad you're all right after everything that happened last night. It certainly could have turned out differently." He paused, seeing me looking at the back of the book again. "*Is* it a local author?"

"As a matter of fact, it is. It's an old friend and former professor of mine. He lives in a retirement community not far from here. It looks like he's written a nonfiction local history for an academic press. A reader requested the purchase. I'd have requested it myself if I'd realized the connection."

Wilson said, "I don't suppose he'd want a book event." There was a good deal of apprehension in his voice.

"Too soon?" I asked lightly.

Wilson nodded. "Quite possibly."

"Fortunately, my friend is the quiet type, and I don't think he'd want an event," I said. "But I'll put a copy in the local author's section."

Wilson's look of relief made me smile. Then he switched briskly to the seed library implementation before heading back to his office.

The quietness of the morning, the smell of the books, the coffee in my travel mug, and the purring cat in front of me all served to put the events of the last week behind me as I settled into my day at the library.

About the Author

Elizabeth writes the Southern Quilting mysteries and Memphis Barbeque mysteries for Penguin Random House and the Myrtle Clover series for Midnight Ink and independently. She blogs at ElizabethSpannCraig.com/blog, named by Writer's Digest as one of the 101 Best Websites for Writers. Elizabeth makes her home in Matthews, North Carolina, with her husband. She's the mother of two.

Sign up for Elizabeth's free newsletter to stay updated on releases:

https://bit.ly/2xZUXqO

This and That

I love hearing from my readers. You can find me on Facebook as Elizabeth Spann Craig Author, on Twitter as elizabethscraig, on my website at elizabethspanncraig.com, and by email at elizabethspanncraig@gmail.com.

Thanks so much for reading my book...I appreciate it. If you enjoyed the story, would you please leave a short review on the site where you purchased it? Just a few words would be great. Not only do I feel encouraged reading them, but they also help other readers discover my books. Thank you!

Did you know my books are available in print and ebook formats? Most of the Myrtle Clover series is available in audio and some of the Southern Quilting mysteries are. Find the audiobooks here: https://elizabethspanncraig.com/audio/

Please follow me on BookBub for my reading recommendations and release notifications.

I'd also like to thank some folks who helped me put this book together. Thanks to my cover designer, Karri Klawiter, for her awesome covers. Thanks to my editor, Judy Beatty for her help. Thanks to beta readers Amanda Arrieta, Rebecca Wahr, Cassie Kelley, and Dan Harris for all of their helpful suggestions and careful reading. Thanks to my ARC readers for helping to spread the word. Thanks, as always, to my family and readers.

Other Works by Elizabeth

Myrtle Clover Series in Order (be sure to look for the Myrtle series in audio, ebook, and print):

Pretty is as Pretty Dies

Progressive Dinner Deadly

A Dyeing Shame

A Body in the Backyard

Death at a Drop-In

A Body at Book Club

Death Pays a Visit

A Body at Bunco

Murder on Opening Night

Cruising for Murder

Cooking is Murder

A Body in the Trunk

Cleaning is Murder

Edit to Death

Hushed Up

A Body in the Attic

Murder on the Ballot

Death of a Suitor

A Dash of Murder

Death at a Diner

A Myrtle Clover Christmas

Murder at a Yard Sale (2023)

Southern Quilting Mysteries in Order:

Quilt or Innocence

Knot What it Seams

Quilt Trip

Shear Trouble

Tying the Knot

Patch of Trouble

Fall to Pieces

Rest in Pieces

On Pins and Needles

Fit to be Tied

Embroidering the Truth

Knot a Clue

Quilt-Ridden

Needled to Death

A Notion to Murder

Crosspatch

Behind the Seams (2023)

The Village Library Mysteries in Order (Debuting 2019):

Checked Out

Overdue

Borrowed Time

Hush-Hush

Where There's a Will

Frictional Characters

Spine Tingling

A Novel Idea

End of Story (2023)

Memphis Barbeque Mysteries in Order (Written as Riley Adams):

Delicious and Suspicious
Finger Lickin' Dead
Hickory Smoked Homicide
Rubbed Out
And a standalone "cozy zombie" novel: Race to Refuge, written as Liz Craig

9 781955 395274